The Greats of Cuttercane

MERCER
UNIVERSITY PRESS

Endowed by
TOM WATSON BROWN
and
THE WATSON-BROWN FOUNDATION, INC.

The Greats of Cuttercane

The Southern Stories

Terry Kay

MERCER UNIVERSITY PRESS

MACON, GEORGIA

MUP / H827 and H827e

© 2011 Terry Kay
Published by Mercer University Press
1400 Coleman Avenue
Macon, Georgia 31207

First Edition

Books published by Mercer University Press are printed on acid-free paper
that meets the requirements of American National Standard for Information
Sciences—Permanence of Paper for Printed Library Materials.

Mercer University Press is a member of Green Press Initiative
(greenpressinitiative.org), a nonprofit organization working to help
publishers and printers increase their use of recycled paper and decrease
their use of fiber derived from endangered forests. This book is printed on
recycled paper.

Library of Congress Cataloging-in-Publication Data
Kay, Terry.
  The greats of cuttercane : stories / Terry Kay. -- 1st ed.
      p. cm.
  ISBN 978-0-88146-249-4 (hardcover : alk. paper) -- ISBN 978-0-88146-250-0 (e-
book)
  1. Short stories. 2. Humorous stories, American. I. Title.
  PS3561.A885G74 2011
  813'.54--dc23
                         2011024538

Also by Terry Kay

Bogmeadow's Wish

The Book of Marie

The Valley of Light

Taking Lottie Home

Special K: The Wisdom of Terry Kay

The Kidnapping of Aaron Greene

The Runaway

Shadow Song

To Whom the Angel Spoke: A Story of the Christmas

To Dance with the White Dog

Dark Thirty

After Eli

The Year the Lights Came On

Again, for Tommie

Contents

Author's Note

In 1962, while on assignment from the *Atlanta Journal* to cover a high school football game in Valdosta (GA), I found myself with idling time and so went into a drug store to browse. There I discovered a book called *Southern Fried*, written by William Price Fox. A collection of short stories, it was, for me, the perfect idling-time purchase.

It also taught me something about southern literature.

Southern literature can be *caricature*-driven as well as *character*-driven, meaning the southern region has some stretch in the way it's identified. A lot of people seem to believe the television show *Beverly Hillbillies* was an accurate account of how people claiming a southern heritage normally behave. Others realize that Harper Lee's *To Kill a Mockingbird* is a more reasonable portrayal.

Let me say I love *Southern Fried*. We have not had a humorist like Fox since—well, Fox. Not even Foxworthy. Yet, I do have some discomfort in knowing that southerners who name their children Bubba are often depicted to outsiders as mutants or comic embarrassments. There's a lot of noticeable (and memorable) surface to such personalities—the way they dress, the places they live, the foods they eat, and especially the way they speak—but if you want to find some depth in one of them, you need to dig as deep as a West Virginia coal-miner.

And, contrary to opinion, southerners are not completely dumb. They know the game of playful deceit, and perform it well. I am familiar with a fellow who wears a white suit and black string tie while visiting in New York City to talk with publishers. It is rumored that he only drinks Mint Juleps on such occasions. Paula Deen (the cooking lady from Savannah) has become a popular caricature of her own personality on her national cooking shows for television, dispensing "Yawls" (sometimes spelled "Y'alls") like the cheap trinkets of a Mardi Gras carnival, but it works for her. And one of the smartest men and ablest writers I know (and I've known him since he was in high school) is Roy Blount, Jr. Roy made his mark and a fine living being an expatriate southerner in New York for many, many years.

As a writer, I've been influenced by a lot of southern authors and Price Fox is chief among them, particularly for my first novel (*The Year the Lights Came On*). A teacher once told me, "Read and learn, Kay. Read and learn." It is, perhaps, the most profound advice I've ever had. And part of that learning is in understanding the great variety of offerings from southern writers. Erskine Caldwell, for example. I greatly admire his *Tobacco Road* and *God's Little Acre*, though I am far more intrigued with his *The Sacrilege of Alan Kent*, one of the most remarkable collections of single paragraphs in American literature. The difference in style and content is startling.

James Dickey's *Deliverance* is a compelling read and the movie version gave the south its most recognizable theme music since *Dixie*, yet the story is a poor delineation of pure Appalachian character. For that, one should pick among the poems of Byron Herbert Reece or read the novels of Wendell Berry and Fred Chappell.

The stretch factor in southern literature is as elastic as the literature of any region of any country in the world—perhaps more so. There's not a scintilla of similarity between Flannery O'Connor and *The Andy Griffith Show*. You wouldn't confuse William Faulkner or Robert Penn Warren with Eugenia Price or Margaret Mitchell.

Still, that stretch intrigues me. For years, I've toyed with a series of short stories, deliberately written in caricature for the sheer fun of writing. I call them the Southern Stories, meaning they're from the sort of exaggeration that crops up when people are trying to out-do one another while sitting around a coffee table in the local café—or wherever they gather. In the writing, I learned there's always an edge of humor and perhaps a dab of poignancy in the stories, but little room for the sweet richness of language. Anything that suggests poetic indulgence puts the style out of sync.

In this book, the characters of the Southern Stories—the *caricatures,* rather—have one thing in common: they are all from the same community, a place somewhere in north Georgia named Cuttercane. Each has been changed by the mysterious power of a sizeable pool of water called Asa's Spring. And each is ordained by the townspeople with a simple phrase: "He's (she's) something, ain't he (she)?"

In small southern communities, such an ordination has meaning, even if that meaning might be cloaked in a touch of absurdity.

Terry Kay

The Greats of Cuttercane

Asa, God, and Woodrow Wilson

The Story of
Asa Holbrook Staggs

The first man to step into the coldwater spring that served as the headwater of Cuttercane Creek was Asa Holbrook Staggs.

Asa fell in, having wandered off Cuttercane Road in search of a shortcut from his whiskey still to his home.

He was drunk.

The time, as Asa would later determine, was approximately seven-thirty in the early evening of Wednesday, November 18, 1914.

He pulled himself from the water, sober, cold, and converted to a new life in the Lord.

Fortuitously, he was not far from the home of the Reverend Horace Carter, a blacksmith who was also the pastor of Cuttercane Baptist Church, and there in Reverend Carter's living room, wet and shivering, Asa made the longest admission of transgressions known in Christendom.

On the following Sunday—with considerable word-of-mouth, pre-service publicity—Asa enthusiastically repeated his confessions before the congregation of the church. According to reports, it was a memorable occasion—loud and circus—and the celebration of Asa's conversion lasted until one-thirty in the afternoon, leaving the worshippers hungry, but energized with gladness.

"Asa's been found," the people yodeled. "Glory to God, brother Asa's come home."

"I have and that's a fact," Asa proclaimed proudly. "But it weren't my doing. It was that water. The Lord's baptized me in it. Took me just as I was, drunk as a skunk, and cleaned me up."

"God's wonderful, ain't He?" cried the people.

"Amen," moaned the Reverend Carter.

To other citizens of Cuttercane—those belonging to other denominations like the Methodists and the Church of God—Asa's conversion was nothing more than humorous blithering, Asa was merely being Asa, and that could mean anything.

"He's not took a bath or been sober in ten years," they said, snickering. "Saved? He wouldn't know being saved from being shaved. He's just addled by what water feels like again."

And: "Ten to one, Asa'll put him a moonshine still in up there. Sell off the makings as Holy Water. That old boy's got more'n his arm up his sleeve."

And: "He's got them Baptists ready to talk in tongues, but, Lord, everybody knows a Baptist has got some strange notions."

Asa heard the talk, mostly from secondhand sources trying to be jokesters or show-offs, but it did not bother him. He held his ground: he had been saved from sin by the waters of the spring and his destiny would be remarkable.

"I was wallowing there in that water, thinking I was drowned," he vowed, "and, sudden-like, I could feel myself being changed. Right there. It was like that water was running all the way through me. Straight through my clothes and skin and insides. That's what it was like. I'm telling you, they's something in that water."

"Maybe he means it," some of the people began to mutter.

"Maybe he does at that."

"Naw. Not Asa. He's never been worth a pinch of owl shit and he won't never be. Lord, he's a Staggs."

Yet, during the months that followed, the doubters became fewer and fewer. Asa ceremoniously destroyed his two whiskey stills, took a job in Joe Cartwright's sawmill, began bathing and shaving every day, and became a devout member of the Cuttercane Baptist Church, renewing a baptism he had taken as a joke at the age of twelve. He was kind to the elderly, playful with children, and, most surprising, he began to take private reading lessons from Rachel Otwell, the young fifth-grade schoolteacher who had a diploma from Mademoiselle Antoinette's Finishing School for Young Ladies of Sophistication, located in Atlanta.

"He's changed, and that's the truth," people began to admit.

"I hear tell he can read his ass off in some of them third-grade books that that Otwell woman's letting him borrow."

"What I hear, too. Somebody said Edgar Bond bet him a dollar he couldn't read a fertilizer sack down at the feed store. Asa took him up on it. Read the name right off the sack. Even got the numbers right—six-eight-six. Said he'd give the dollar he won to the church since he didn't take to gambling, being the Baptist that he was."

"Shows what a man can do, he sets his mind to it."

"It does. No doubt about it."

"Yessir, that boy's something. He sure is."

But there was more to Asa's new life than talk and reading lessons. He used the first money he earned from his work at Joe Cartwright's sawmill as a down payment on the spring that had cleansed his life of sin. The agreement with Jewell Proudfoot, a Cherokee Indian, also included one hundred paces of land in all directions from the exact center of the spring.

"That's so I can maybe put up a little shelter out there, in case the church wants to use it for baptizing," Asa said thoughtfully. "A little place for the ladies and old people to stand under in case it starts to rain."

"Maybe we ought to think that out," advised the Reverend Carter. "I'm not saying that's not good baptizing water, but it's hard to get in to where that spring is. Got all that river cane growing around there."

"I aim to clean it out, Preacher," Asa said. "Maybe put a road in, even if I have to shovel it out by myself."

"Well, you're a kind man to go to all that trouble, Asa," the Reverend Carter replied. "Lord'll bless you for it. You'll see."

"Lord's done blessed me already, Preacher," declared Asa. "Made me new. That's what I am, Preacher. New. N-E-W, new. New as the morning."

Jewell Proudfoot did not think of Asa as a made-over Christian; Jewell thought of Asa as a fool. He did not understand white men, though he had married a white woman, Sara Willis, in 1897, and had worked with white men all his life. Jewell believed Asa was as ridiculous as Benjamin Cutter, the first white settler of the region. Jewell's great grandfather had saved Benjamin Cutter's life in 1807 and Benjamin Cutter had rewarded his Indian friend with a Christian name—Obadiah Proudfoot—and a sizeable tract of land that he had stolen from the Cherokees by the declaration of a bogus deed. The land included an impressive ridge that Benjamin Cutter called Proudfoot Hill. The spring was at the base of Proudfoot Hill.

The reason Jewell felt particularly triumphant in his agreement with Asa was the thick stand of wild river cane that grew around the spring. To Jewell, the cane was as worthless as weeds, except for fishing poles. Yet, it was Jewell's observation that white men were impressed with cane. His great grandfather had described how Benjamin Cutter had constructed a house of cane, woven like a basket around slender pine poles that had been cut, stripped, and stuck into the ground every two feet. The house supposedly lasted less than a year, but it was unique and the settlers who followed Benjamin Cutter into the region called the area Cutter's Cane, which was later amended by a Britisher mapping the territory. Cuttercane, as a single word, had a distinctive, lyrical personality, the Britisher proposed, and the name had lasted, though none of the settlers could say it the way the Britisher said it.

"White men," Jewell said to his wife in a sad, confused voice. "Damned if I know how they think. It's a good thing our boy has got

Indian blood in him." Their boy was named Newell. To the people of Cuttercane, Newell Proudfoot also had a lot of Devil in him.

And Asa said to Joe Cartwright, "Jewell don't know what he sold. Way it is with Indians. Some of them don't got the sense God give a hog. No wonder most of them moved off to Oklahoma. They couldn't make it in the hills."

His bargain with Jewell Proudfoot was, for Asa, the crowning moment of his life. He was a landowner. No one in his family had ever owned land. In celebration, he cleared away the thickets of cane and mountain laurel surrounding the spring and then widened the pool of water until it was thirty feet in diameter and five feet deep in the middle. When he finished his work, Asa renewed himself by stripping naked and walking into the frigid waters. He stood, unmoving, arms folded in a religious gesture across his chest, until his skin began to tint purple from the cold.

He did not know it, but Asa's intended ritual of privacy had been witnessed by Jewell Proudfoot, who was hiding, Indian-style, under the shade of a beech tree on Proudfoot Hill. Jewell could not understand why a man would work so laboriously over a small pond of water when creeks and rivers were abundant.

"Asa's not right in the head," Jewell said to the men of Cuttercane.

"Not if he's standing around freezing his nuts off in ice water," the men of Cuttercane concurred.

"Sad, what happens to some people," the men added.

"It is. That's right. Makes me feel sorry for Asa. It's a good thing his mama and daddy has gone on to their reward. They'd be stressed."

Though Asa heard the murmurings and saw pity in the eyes of the men and many of the women, he was not discouraged. "It's as close to the Resurrection in the Bible of anything I ever heard tell of," he said to the Reverend Carter, while the Reverend Carter hammered a shoe onto the hoof of Asa's mule.

"Sounds that way to me, Asa," said the Reverend Carter. He dropped the mule's hoof from the vise of his knees and looked kindly at Asa. "You got to remember, Asa, they was them that mocked after our Lord Jesus."

"And Peter, the Rock," Asa added profoundly.

"And Peter," echoed the Reverend Carter.

"They can laugh all they want to," Asa declared. "It don't matter. I been saved."

"Praise God for it," whispered the Reverend Carter.

The only person who seemed deeply bothered by the teasing of Asa was Rachel Otwell. She had been astonished by his skill at reading and had begun to feel a warm attachment for him, even if his very presence exemplified everything Mademoiselle Antoinette had warned her girls to avoid. She did not like seeing him so willing to be ridiculed. "Maybe you should be less enthusiastic about the spring, Asa," she advised. "That way people won't go around slandering you."

"Sister Rachel, they're the ones to be pitied, not me," Asa told her. "Someday, they'll know it."

"But, Asa, they're making fun."

"And God bless them, Sister Rachel. Makes them happy. God bless them all. It don't bother me none. You remember that fellow Job, the one in the Bible? Well, that's me—Job. Don't make no difference what they say, I can take it."

"I just don't like what they're doing," Rachel sighed.

"The Lord's leading me, Sister Rachel. You'll see. They's something waiting for me. The Lord'll let me know."

Rachel struggled to keep her tears from flooding. She thought: Such a good man, but maybe he is afflicted with some mental imbalance.

Rachel did not know Asa's destiny was closing in on him, a destiny that would involve Woodrow Wilson and a Mexican bandit.

Until 1912, no one in Cuttercane had ever cared for the world outside the foothills of the Great Smoky Mountains. The world outside had always been embroiled in distant and unnecessary quarrels and such senseless afflictions were like diseases that floated on air. A single carrier could destroy an entire town.

In 1912, things changed. Oscar John Norris, the town doctor, visited Washington, D.C. and there met Woodrow Wilson, the Democrat's nominee for President of the United States. Dr. Oscar, as he was known, was impressed with Wilson and made certain that Cuttercane was also impressed—an easy enough task, since most people in the county owed Dr. Oscar for medical services. Not a single person dared speak in favor of the Republican candidate, Charles Evans Hughes, and when Wilson was elected, Dr. Oscar was so elated he hosted a party to celebrate. Every citizen in Cuttercane attended and on that night, following a stirring speech on Americanism by Dr. Oscar, Cuttercane joined the outside world as dedicated Wilsonites.

Asa had been one of the few in the Cuttercane valley not impressed by the election of Woodrow Wilson; he had been too drunk to care. And after his conversion in 1914, he was too busy pondering God's calling to worry about politics—until the night of the curious dream. In his dream, the Lord and Woodrow Wilson appeared to Asa in a vision, walking arm in arm across the foot of his bed. The next day, Asa announced to the Reverend Carter that he would join the United States army.

9

The Reverend Carter was astonished. "What for, Asa?" he asked. "Nobody I know of from around here ever joined the army."

"I'm doing it for the Lord God Almighty," Asa proclaimed giddily. "He said it in my dream, said, 'Get up from there, Asa. Get up off that bed and go join Brother Wilson's army.' That's what He said, Preacher, clear as day, clear as I been hearing you."

"You say Woodrow Wilson was with Him?" the Reverend Carter inquired curiously.

"Right beside Him, close up," answered Asa. "Almost on the bed post, like he was leaning up against it."

"President Wilson say anything?" asked the Reverend Carter.

Asa shook his head. "Not a word. The Lord was doing all the talking, but it could have been that President Wilson nodded once or twice. I couldn't see him too good. They was all this light around the Lord."

"Well, Brother Asa, I'm not about to go arguing with the Lord God Almighty," the Reverend Carter said. "You sure He was talking about the army?"

"Clear as a bell, Preacher."

"The United States Army?"

"Now that you mention it, He didn't say United States," Asa admitted. "Not in them words, not that I remember, but that's what I'm thinking He meant, having the president there with Him. Besides, they was something like a whisper—no, more like the cooing of a bird, maybe a dove—and it sounded to me like they could have been saying *'United States, United States.'* Soft-like, I mean."

The Reverend Carter had never before counseled a circumstance as puzzling. He squeezed his face in a theological frown and nodded slowly, as if in deep thought. Then he said, "The Lord speaks, you got to listen, Asa. The Lord knows better'n you and me."

"That's right," Asa replied seriously.

"Sounded like a bird, you say? Maybe like a dove?"

"Could have been angels," Asa suggested. "They was angels all over the place, up near the ceiling, floating around. I could hear them harmonizing, like they was at a church singing."

"Wish I could of heard that, Brother Asa," the Reverend Carter said with longing.

"I wish you could of, too, Preacher. I sure do," Asa said. "Praise the Lord God Almighty. I can feel Him pulling on me. I can feel it happening. He's leading me down His path."

"You almost got me feeling it, Brother Asa," the Reverend Carter moaned.

In the seesaw of public opinion about Asa's religious insight, there were many who did not think it was the Lord who was pulling, or leading, him. The Lord surely had better things to do than take up His time with a Staggs. It was late 1915. Sparrows were dropping out of the skies everywhere. People were being killed in automobiles and airplanes. There was still talk of the Titanic. Germany was at war with anyone who stood in its path. President Wilson was busy trying to keep the peace. The Lord was needed for serious business. Asa Holbrook Staggs was not a priority on the Lord's schedule. Asa Holbrook Staggs was just plain crazy.

"All that drinking for all them years," the people said. "Burnt up his brain."

"Puts you in mind of Old Lady Witherspoon, don't it? Used to crawl up on top of her barn and hold on to the weather vane and crow like a rooster. Poor old soul."

"I hear tell Old Man Witherspoon tried to shoot her down one day."

"Missed her."

"Never was much of a shot. I been hunting with him."

"Both of them used to be bad to drink, what I hear. Somebody said the old man made it on that branch that run behind his house."

"Stuff'll rot your brains out, you drink too much of it."

"Don't want to talk bad about nobody, but Old Lady Witherspoon must of had her share."

"Don't know about that, but Asa has. I guarantee it."

And the talk from the citizens of Cuttercane greatly distressed Rachel Otwell. She said, in a begging voice, "Oh, Asa, why?"

"The Lord knows, Sister Rachel," said Asa in answer. "He wants me marching for him in his army. I guess He's got His reason."

Less than a year later, in late summer of 1916, Asa was in Mexico with General John J. Pershing, chasing after Pancho Villa, who had raided the village of Columbus, New Mexico, leaving death and destruction in his wake.

It was there that God revealed Asa's destiny.

Or so Asa would believe.

On one eventful night, Asa was credited with personally preventing a surprise assault by Villa's troops against the encampment of American soldiers.

The offical dispatch praised Private Staggs for ". . . recognizing a danger and acting to alert his fellow soldiers by causing confusion among the enemy and scattering their horses."

The truth was less dramatic.

Asa had wandered off to pray and contemplate his destiny, as he did nightly, and he had prayed himself into sleep on a patch of scrub brush. When he awoke, near sunrise, he was surrounded by waiting horses of Villa's troops. Sleepy, unaware of the horses or the men, and being overstuffed on beans for his dinner of the night before, Asa stood, stretched, yawned, and broke wind.

The horses spooked at the sudden, harsh eruption and two Mexicans fired wildly in Asa's direction. Asa dove into the bushes and buried his face in the sand and covered his head with his hands. He did not move until the horses and the Mexicans had disappeared in a confusion of gunfire, swearing, and the aroused battle cry of American soldiers in spirited pursuit. A captured Mexican later spoke of the lone American who had tried to assassinate Pancho Villa with a cannon. Asa was quickly identified as that soldier and was presented to General Pershing.

"It was the Lord that done it," Asa declared to the general. "It weren't me. It was the Lord moving in me."

A stunned General Pershing, upon hearing the truth from his officers, reportedly said, "Give the man a medal."

And a medal was found and awarded and Asa was dispatched with a senior officer to Washington, D.C., where he proudly described what he called the Voice from Within, a phrase that understanding reporters kindly omitted from their stories. He also attended a reception to meet President Wilson and, later, traveled to a tent meeting in Virginia to meet Billy Sunday. Billy Sunday was the only person who seemed to understand Asa. "Shows that God uses all his vessels for good," Billy supposedly proclaimed.

A month later, the United States Army granted Private Asa Holbrook Staggs a permanent furlough to return to Cuttercane, Georgia, and there spend the rest of his service commitment in promoting religious patriotism. Getting Asa out of the army was considered by many as the only substantial victory the United States could claim in its undeclared war against the elusive Pancho Villa.

Asa returned to Cuttercane a hero, wearing a hero's medal. He received a hero's welcome. He delivered a rambling hero's speech about God and Woodrow Wilson and Billy Sunday, ending it with a reminder that it all had started when he fell into the cold waters of a hidden spring at the foot of Proudfoot Hill, drunk and worthless as a man could get. "I been saying I was intended for something ever since then, and the Lord proved it, didn't He?"

It was after Asa's exaggerated speech that citizens began to ask his permission to bathe in Asa's Spring, as it had been named by the believers of the Cuttercane Baptist Church. Asa was deeply moved by the sincerity of the requests. He knew he had fulfilled his own destiny in Mexico, but he knew also that others might find a blessing in the mysterious waters bubbling up from deep in the ground.

"The land belongs to me," Asa said, "but the water belongs to everybody."

"You're a kind man, Asa Holbrook Staggs," Rachel Otwell told him tenderly. "A hero and a kind man. You're a credit to all of us."

"Just doing what the Lord wants done," Asa said philosophically.

And one by one, the people of Cuttercane began to wade into Asa's Spring, each expecting the rush of a miracle that awaited them in clear, cold water.

The first to experience a change in his life was Ellis Goodbread, who learned three weeks after bathing in Asa's Spring that he had inherited a home and a surprisingly large sum of money as the only living relative of a silversmith in Boston.

"That's something," the people said in awe as Ellis praised the wonder of Asa's Spring.

"Asa's been right all along," the people acknowledged. "Ellis Goodbread was as poor as they come."

"Just shows you got to be patient. No need to be rushing things."

The second to benefit from Asa's Spring was Lucille Andrews, who became pregnant one week after wading fully clothed into the icy waters.

"You talk about something, that's something," the people said in stunned voices. "Word is, Lucille's been wanting a baby for ten years and nothing's happened. Guess maybe that's the way it works. Guess maybe that spring water helps you do what it don't look like you can do. Like Asa. Asa was sorry as they come. And Ellis, not having a penny to rub against a nickel, and now Lucille."

"Could be, but I'm don't want my woman nowheres near that spring if they's babies in the water. We got seven already."

To Asa, the reports of Ellis Goodbread and Lucille Andrews were affirmations that his spring contained elements God had hidden from all mankind since the beginning of time. In his thinking, it was possible that Cuttercane was located where the Garden of Eden had been, and Asa's Spring was the original drinking and bathing water for Adam and Eve, a theory he proposed one Sunday to the congregation of the Cuttercane Baptist Church. To many, his words were as inspired and as inspiring as anything from the Old Testament and several spoke in awe of what it could mean, living next to the Garden of Eden. Among the instant believers was the Reverend Carter.

"The Bible don't say exactly where the Garden was," the Reverend Carter mused. "It don't say Paris, France, or Rome, Italy, or Spain or England or any of them other places, although I always imagined it to be somewhere around Jerusalem. Far as I know, they's never been a road map showing it, and they weren't no signposts in them days. Just having Adam and Eve and then Cain and Abel, they didn't need things like that. They knew where they was and they weren't expecting company that I know of. Maybe Brother Asa's right. Maybe the Garden of Eden was right here in Cutter County."

And the members of the congregation said among themselves, "Could have been, come to think of it. We got a lot of apple trees around here."

After Ellis Goodbread's and Lucille Andrews' indisputable experiences, Asa's Spring was used for everything from curing warts to growing hair on balding men, all without success. It became the baptismal pool for every church practicing immersion in the Cuttercane Valley. And as the fervor for miracles intensified, a number of minor events were credited to the mysterious properties of the water. Norris Redwine recovered suddenly from a respiratory illness that had struck him a week after his name had been pulled from the lottery for World War One. Otto Harper, blind in one eye, won a marksman contest shooting for a turkey against a traveling Frenchman named DuBrow. Jake Gainous awoke from a dead sleep, on instinct, and discovered a live coal that had tumbled from the fireplace burning slowly into the heart-of-pine floor. Another ten minutes, Jake vowed, and the whole house would have been in flame. And Darby Sellers, who was on the confirmed side of ugly, persuaded Glanell Phillips, who was remarkably beautiful, to marry him, prompting a rush of every bachelor in Cuttercane to leap into Asa's Spring. "If Darby can get Glanell, I, by God, ought to have Mary Pickford eating out of my hand," the bachelors were saying with excitement.

Asa, who had married Rachel Otwell in June of 1918, listened tirelessly to the testimony of those who praised the waters of his spring for every small improvement in their lives, though he realized there was as much exaggeration as truth in the reports.

"They testing the Lord," Asa said fretfully.

"People believe what they need to believe, Asa," Rachel counseled.

"Maybe so, but they testing the Lord," Asa argued. "I been hearing all this talk, but they's been nobody like Ellis and Lucille in a long time. Maybe they's too many people going out there. Maybe the Lord don't want so many people wading around in His water."

"Don't worry about it, Asa. You'll just make your heartburn act up."

"Uh-huh," Asa mumbled, rubbing his chest absently.

Asa's longing for a spectacular demonstration that his spring had not lost is power was finally answered in late 1919 by a frail, shy man named Samuel Roswell Martin, who seldom spoke to anyone because he stuttered. Samuel Roswell Martin had had an intense dream about the spring and the following day, a cool September morning, he walked into the water as his wife, Ruth, and their three children watched from the bed of their two-mule wagon.

As Ruth would later tell the story, Samuel waded to the middle of the spring, his face twitching from the cold. He then kneeled and began to sink slowly beneath the surface until she could see nothing but the mat of his hair floating on the surface like a wad of dead grass. Suddenly, his body shot upward and Samuel rose from the water, his hair and face glistening in the morning sunlight, and he opened his mouth and he began to speak in a voice of thunder, each word as clipped and precise as a touring Chautauqua actor.

"Near scared me to death," Ruth confessed to the Reverend Carter. "The children started bawling and holding on to me, but Samuel come up out of that water smiling and saying, 'Don't be scared of nothing. The Lord's took away my old tongue and give me a new one.'"

Asa was so elated by the miracle of Samuel Roswell Martin, the stutterer, he invited Samuel and the Reverend Carter to his home and he urged Samuel to talk, to read, to recite John 3:16, and he marveled at the rich bass of Samuel's voice.

"The Lord wants something out of you," Asa advised.

"Like what?" asked Samuel.

"I'd say He wants you to go preach the Word," Asa said. He turned to the Reverend Carter. "You think that's right, Preacher? Samuel ought to go out and preach the Word."

"Seems that way to me," the Reverend Carter agreed.

And so it happened that Samuel sold his farm, took up the Bible, and drove away with his family in their two-mule wagon. Years later, he was considered the greatest evangelist in America and his sermon on the holy waters of Asa's Spring was regarded as a classic testimonial to the power of faith.

And the people of Cuttercane said, "You want to talk about something, it's Samuel Martin. Him being tongue-tied and then getting a voice like that. He's something, he is."

After Samuel Roswell Martin, there were no more great miracles from Asa's Spring, though the spring continued to receive credit for any success—from gambling to romance—that the citizens of Cuttercane enjoyed. Yet, those who expected the kind of miracles reported in the Bible were disappointed. It was as though Samuel had removed the spring's curative elements, had soaked them up in his skin and hair, and had marched away with them.

As the years passed, the believers disappeared to death or to distance. All except Asa. Into his old age, beyond the death of his wife Rachel, Asa continued to keep the banks of the spring cleared of mountain laurel and river cane. He continued to immerse himself in the spring, anointing himself, believing he could feel the water seeping into his skin and muscle and bone, flowing into and through him, cleansing tissue and soul.

Newer citizens of Cuttercane, coming to the valley over concrete highways, listened to old tales of Asa and Asa's Spring and snickered in a haughty, put-down fashion.

"Nothing in that old waterhole but lizards and trash," they said among themselves.

"People must have been crazy back in those days."

"Must have been. That old man Staggs looks it. Have you ever seen him?"

"Once or twice. Got a crazy spark in his eye."

"Well, I know of people who still go down to that spring and stick their toe in it, just in case."

"Don't see that it hurts anything."

"I guess not."

After Asa died in 1967, the mountain laurel and river cane grew again around the bowl of the spring. Still, there were narrow paths leading to it and still there were people who waded into its waters, carrying secret wishes to be different.

In 1970, the Historical Society of the South erected a granite marker near the spring. The marker read:

In Honor of

Asa Holbrook Staggs

One of the Greats of Cuttercane

Let those who enter these waters

Make ready for the fate

That will come to mark their name

It was fair warning—for believers and for fools.

Unfortunately, there were more fools than believers, and Asa's Spring did not seem to know the difference.

The World's Last Heavyweight
Lard Watermelon Bout

The Story of
Newell Proudfoot

The reason Newell Proudfoot challenged the Prichard twins to a lard watermelon fight—according to Newell—was because the twins, Dwaine and David, had insulted Lucky Teasley and Newell was fond of Lucky.

Yet, truth be known, Lucky was more an excuse than a reason. Newell simply did not like the long-haired Prichard twins.

The Prichard twins were young—nineteen in years—and mean.

Especially Dwaine.

Dwaine was meaner than David.

Dwaine wore the junior version of a Jim Bowie hunting knife strapped to his belt. Once he had used the knife to cut open a man who worked for his father's construction company. It was an unpunished act of violence, smoothed over by the power and bank account of Quinton Prichard, leaving Dwaine to believe that everyone in Eden County was in fear of him. And he was mostly right.

Except for Newell.

Newell did not fear anyone, which was why his decision to come out of retirement for a lard watermelon fight was greeted with rejoicing by the male population of Eden County.

The men said:

"Great Goda'mighty, Newell's gonna fight again."

The men shouted:

"Newell's taking on the Prichard twins. Both of them at the same time, and he never done that before."

The men chortled:

"Newell's got to be crazy. He's old as Jack's goat, and them boys is meaner'n snakes, especially Dwaine."

"Don't mean nothing," the arguers argued. "You got any money, you better put it on Newell."

"When they doing it?"

"Tonight, out at Sorrow's Pond."

And the men hooted for joy.

23

It was Saturday, late summer of 1950, a day of heat floating on humidity. The incident with Lucky Teasley had taken place in early afternoon in Ira Folley's Tavern, which was located on Highway 17, just north of Edenville. Considering the history of confrontations that had occurred in Ira's Tavern, the disagreement had been a minor one. Dwaine, half-drunk on mountain whiskey and beer chasers, had called Lucky a "poor-assed excuse of a nigger" and Ira had taken it as an indirect insult on his establishment, since Lucky had been employed by the tavern for more than a dozen years.

Ira had yanked his baseball bat from the counter beneath his cash register and had ordered Dwaine out of his tavern.

Dwaine had pulled his knife from its sheath and had grabbed Lucky around the neck and placed the knife blade against Lucky's throat. "Put the bat down, old man, or I'll slice his throat like I was peeling a tomato," Dwaine had snarled.

Everyone in Ira's Tavern had gone motionless—everyone except Newell, who was playing pool with Boggie Hazlehurst. Newell had handed his cue stick to Boggie and had crossed the room to position himself between Dwaine and Ira.

"What you want, Half-Breed?" Dwaine had snapped.

"That's a friend of mine you got," Newell had said in a low, even voice. "I know his daddy. You let go of him, and do it right now."

Dwaine had snickered.

"You put a nick on him and you gonna have to cut me like I was a scalded boar in a hog-killing," Newell had warned calmly.

"You better start oinking," Dwaine had said in his defiant way of showing off. "You ain't man enough to take me on."

No one had moved, no one had spoken, leaving silence to hang in the air like an invisible weight.

And then Newell had said, "Tell you what, Dwaine, why don't you meet me for a lard watermelon fight out at Sorrow's Pond. We'll see who's the man." He had paused and smiled. "Bring David. Let's make it fair."

Dwaine had relaxed and pushed Lucky away from him. A sneer had covered his face. Because Newell had retired from competition years earlier, Dwaine had never seen a lard watermelon bout, yet he knew Newell had introduced the game—if it could be called a game—to Eden County thirty years earlier, claiming it was an ancient Indian ceremony used for settling tribal differences in a more civilized manner than war.

The story was, in fact, a wonderful lie. As a young man in the north Georgia community of Cuttercane, Newell had watched one day from the camouflage of a cane thicket as children of farm families played a harmless game in Asa's Spring. A watermelon would be floated to the middle of the pool and the first person to push the watermelon to shore was the winner.

Newell had merely amended the rules, applying the made-up mystique of Indian lore by calling it the Sport of Chiefs. The way Newell described it, the game was played in the style of a cockfight, with human adversaries in a water pit, clawing at one another in a vicious, brutal struggle over a watermelon that had been coated in pig lard, making it too slick to hold, while men huddled like thieves on the shoreline to do their wagering and to beg for drownings.

Newell had retired undefeated in 1940. He was, he said, too old for the danger. He had smoked too many tins of Prince Albert tobacco, consumed too much rotgut whiskey, and spent himself in the bellies of too many loose and willing women. "Can't do it no more," he had bemoaned. "My reflexes is shot. It's a young man's game and it's been a long time since I was young."

Dwaine Prichard knew all of this. If he had ever been secretly in awe of anyone, it was Newell Proudfoot. Newell was a slender six-three, but looked taller in his felt hat with the buzzard's feather. He wore cowboy shirts with pearl buttons and his jeans were held up by a hand-tooled leather belt containing a silver buckle the size of a coffee saucer. Newell's belt buckle was the envy of every man in Eden County.

Newell was part-Cherokee—one-half by his reasoning, since his daddy, Jewell Proudfoot, had been a full-blood—and his face, at his age, had developed the fine-line symmetrical cracking of red-clay land in the fifth week of a drought. His skin was the color of a rosy bronze. His eyes were small and dark, like the eyes of a bird. "Indian eyes," he explained to anyone who would listen. "Got them from my daddy's side. He could see like a hawk on the fly, and my eyes is better. I can count the flapping of a hummingbird's wings."

Dwaine's unspoken admiration of Newell was worthy of the envy. Newell not only looked Indian, he behaved Indian—at least what he called Indian. As a child, reared in the forests of the Cuttercane Valley, he had imagined himself as a Cherokee warrior trained in the arts of animal stalking, of bow and arrow hunting, of reading the signs of nature and, curiously, of cowboy fighting, though the only cowboys in Georgia were under ten years of age and shot pistols made of chinaberry sticks.

Newell did not care what people said about the conflict of cowboys and Indians in the Wild West, or what they showed in moving picture theaters. In northeast Georgia the cowboys never won. Newell terrorized them. Once, he staked Tommy Childers to a mound of ants and scalped him with a pair of scissors. Tommy had made the mistake of pretending to be a Texas Ranger.

The people of Cuttercane called him devilish and laughed at such antics.

The people of Eden County, where Newell had settled in his early twenties, did not laugh at his antics.

As a man, Newell had taken up drinking, only to discover his tolerance for hard liquor was embarrassingly low and his judgment had a noticeable lack of wisdom. What he had practiced as a child, he performed as a man. He had been known to attack—with disturbing frequency—the entire city of Edenville. Dressed in full Indian regalia he had ordered from a costume company based in Dallas, Texas, he would smear war paint of black shoe polish over his nose and forehead and then he would mount a white mule named Fanny and go looking for the Chief of the Pale Faces, whose name was Angus Seals, the sheriff of Eden County. Angus had learned to stay out of sight until Newell passed out and fell off Fanny. "Best way to handle the fool," was the way Angus defended his tactics. "Better that than having a arrow stuck up my butt."

Over time, Newell's behavior improved and when he finally took the oath against hard liquor in 1935, he became a model citizen and head of the town's Sanitation Department, a respectable position that he handled with confidence and pride.

Still, the old stories remained, especially the stories of his prowess as the World's Heavyweight Lard Watermelon Champion. Newell Proudfoot was a man's man, the people said, the descendent of a Cherokee chief who avoided the Trail of Tears by hiding in the caves of mountains among a tribe of bears. Like his ancestor, Newell was strong and fearless and, most importantly, he was undefeated in the Sport of the Chiefs.

It was being undefeated that Dwaine could not accept.

"You got it, big boy," Dwaine had snapped in response to Newell's challenge. "You think you scaring me, you whistling *Dixie*. Bring it on. You ready, I'm ready." He had laughed a cackling laugh.

"Don't forget David," Newell had said calmly. "Wouldn't want it to look one-sided."

Dwaine had laughed again. He had turned to David. "You hear that, brother?" he had yodeled. "Me'n you both. You reckon this broke-down old half-breed done lost what little sense he had?"

"Yeah," David had answered timidly. David had doubts. David was afraid of Newell Proudfoot.

"Fine, Dwaine, fine," Newell had said quietly. "Call me what you want to. I just hope you remember to show up."

By the time the sound wave of news about the lard watermelon fight had rushed from Edenville into the farm communities of Eden County, fact had expanded into the gore of fiction. Lucky Teasley, it was declared, had had his throat slit by Dwaine and Newell had vowed to avenge the death by drowning Dwaine in Sorrow's Pond. People were livid with rage. Even those who barely knew Lucky told tales of friendship with him, tinted in sadness over his pitiful condition in life. Lucky had been born with a spinal deformity and when he served beer and hotdogs in Ira's Tavern, he drug his left leg and pumped his elbows in a pulling motion, like a featherless chicken trying to fly. Anyone who would pick on a man of Lucky's handicap was a natural-born son of a bitch and deserved drowning, and it didn't have the first thing to do with Lucky being colored; a put-down man needed stand-up help. Truth be known, Dwaine was fortunate that it was Newell who had stepped forward, the men of Eden County allowed. "If I'd of been there, I'd of whipped his ass on the spot," the men suggested boldly. "White or colored. Don't matter. You don't go around treating the downtrodden like that."

An hour before sundown, the men of Edenville and Eden County began gathering at Sorrow's Pond, assuring a waterside view by the staking of their physical presence. Some brought chairs or picnic benches. A few carried shotguns in the event of finding a snake sunning itself on a log.

28

"Old Newell must be pissed off," they chattered among themselves.

"He ought to be. Him and Lucky was good buddies."

"Too bad about Lucky getting his throat cut."

"Who said that? I come by the tavern on my way out here. Him and Ira was loading the pickup with beer and what looked like a pan of hotdogs."

"Well, be damned. I heard tell Lucky got killed."

"What I heard was he pissed his pants."

"Don't matter none. Newell's going in the water. That's what I'm out here to see. Been a long time."

"I'll take two-to-one on Newell, whatever anybody's got."

"Ten on that. Newell's getting old. Must be fifty, if he's a day."

Newell Proudfoot was exactly fifty, the same age as Sorrow's Pond, which had been constructed in 1900 by Judge Ridgeway Sorrow, using convict labor. In those years, Ridgeway Sorrow had been known as the Jailing Judge. After the construction of his pond, he became so benevolent in his rulings that a new Sunday School addition to the Edenville Presbyterian Church was dedicated in his honor.

Still, those who saw it knew Sorrow's Pond was more than a pool of water. It was one of God's omissions in his seven-day rush with the matter of creation, an omission that Ridgeway Sorrow had recognized and corrected. "It weren't God's fault," Ridgeway Sorrow was credited with saying. "I just had more time to look at it than he did."

It was not a large lake. Ten acres, maybe. Twelve at the most. And for those in the know—those who had the advantage of history taken from the gossip of family, the kind of history unspoiled by fact—the magic of Sorrow's Pond was from its headwaters of Asa's Spring in the north Georgia foothill community of Cuttercane.

As the water left Asa's Spring and trickled southward, it picked up the add-on of small branches and wet-weather springs and rain runoff until it became a silver string of mountain-cold water flowing into the green bubble of Sorrow's Pond. The green of the lake was the color of pale jade, richer and darker in the channel stream, clean and clear against a heavily wooded shoreline dotted by outcroppings of granite that jutted over the water. There was a saying among locals: "It's pretty enough to make you cry."

Sorrow's Pond was narrow. Its water bowl above the dam was no deeper than twenty feet, but the free-running stream had kept the flooring of the pond from caking in mud. The only collection of silt was a thin coating in the bottom of the bowl. The water was wood sweet, a delicacy to the lips of those who cupped it in the palms of their hands. And it had power. Or, supposedly so. A congregation of hard-shell Baptists used Sorrow's Pond for foot-washing and baptizing because of the stories about Asa's Spring having God's special curative properties. "It's where God washed his own feet," the believers said of Asa's Spring, "and we got the runoff right here in Sorrow's Pond." There were others—Methodists, Presbyterians, Southern Baptists—who questioned the authority of such a revelation because it had the haughtiness of the Catholics. Besides, it seemed unlikely that God would permit one of his holy places to be desecrated by Newell Proudfoot defending his standing as the World's Heavyweight Lard Watermelon Champion, and Newell had never competed at any other location—for good reason: he had a historic association with Asa's Spring. Once it had belonged to his great-grandfather, before the Cherokee had been rousted from the mountains by Andrew Jackson's troops, yet by some miracle of treaty or trading that puzzled Newell, the property had remained in his family until sold by his father, who was named Jewell Proudfoot, to a man named Asa Holbrook Staggs. History had it that Asa Holbrook Staggs had discovered the unique properties of the spring, though

Newell was convinced his father and grandfather and great grandfather had always known of the magic of the water.

To Newell, the water carried the ghost-history of his past, flowing from a sacred pit of time. He believed it would always protect him. In Newell's thinking, a man could not drown in the waters of his soul.

Ira arrived at sundown, driving his pickup, side gates up, covered with canvas. His face was puffed and red and perspiration flowed over his jowls and down his chin. Lucky was in the cab, deep in the seat, peering over the open window frame, a mix of smile and confusion and fear etched into his face.

Boggie Hazelhurst and Frank White and a half-dozen other men wandered over to the truck.

"Took you long enough," Boggie said to Ira as Ira unhooked the tailgate chain.

"Well, by God, Boggie, I had to load up," snapped Ira. "Weren't nobody left at the tavern but me and Lucky and Lucky's still shaking so bad he ain't worth a pinch of owl shit."

"You gonna be the judge?" asked Frank.

"Of course I am," answered Ira. "You see anybody else that knows how to do it? Didn't I do it the last time, back in forty? You was there. You and Boggie both. You seen me make Newell quit hitting that old boy after he got him to the bank."

"Ira, you was passed out cold when Newell pulled that fellow out of the water," Boggie said dryly.

Ira glared at Boggie. He said, "Boggie, you full of horse hockey, you know that? But that don't make no difference. I'm judging and I can tell you that nothing's gonna happen until every drinking man here buys up." He dropped the tailgate of the truck and began to pull boxes from under damp wheat straw and canvas. "Boys," he announced proudly, "this new stuff's so right it's got to be kept cool,

31

just like ni-tro. I guarantee it'll take warts off a bear's butt or put two inches on your pecker, depending on what you chase it with."

Frank laughed easily. "What if you take it straight, Ira?"

"Son, you'd take on Joe Louis and two New Orleans' whores at the same time and never feel nothing," Ira replied seriously, pouring from a gallon jar into a paper cup held by Lucky. "If I was you, I'd stick with sweet milk."

Frank laughed again. He took the cup from Lucky.

"Who's got the watermelon?" Ira asked.

"Peavy Eaton," Frank said. "He picked a truckload yesterday."

"Who's got the lard?"

"Peavy," Frank replied. "He brought along a five-gallon can."

"Well, good Lord, somebody ought to buy Peavy a drink," Ira suggested enthusiastically.

"Let Peavy buy his own drink," a voice chortled. "He's got the money. He's over there selling watermelons out of his pickup."

The crowd had reached a carnival's frenzy by the first sheet of blue-black night. Campfires dotted the shoreline of Sorrow's Pond. Merriment buzzed in the air like the music of insects. Oddsmakers barked like dogs chasing rabbits. Money slipped from hand to hand. Lucky dashed about, dragging his bad leg, pouring corn whiskey and beer and serving hotdogs slathered in chili. Ira stood in the bed of his truck, directing traffic.

The Prichard twins had arrived, outfitted in swimming trunks and wearing matching cowboy hats over the train of their long hair. They were sitting on a blanket beneath a water oak, accepting advice from men who had seen Newell Proudfoot many times in Sorrow's Pond.

The men said: "Swims like a snake, boys. Quick as a bass spitting a hook."

"Watch him when he goes under and stays down. Got that Indian blood in him. You'd swear he's got gills, and when he comes up, he's dead on that watermelon."

"Keep away from them fingernails of his. They's like hooks."

"I hear tell his toenails is longer."

"If I was y'all, I'd have one of me keeping Newell busy and the other one of me would be after that watermelon."

"No way you can just grab that thing. No sir. It'll slip out of your hands like a swallowed oyster. You got to push it, get it near the bank, then throw it up on the shore. That's the way Newell does it."

"You get close enough, kick him in the gonads. That's what he'll be doing to you."

"Yeah, you don't got no rules to this sport."

Dwaine listened with a smug smile. He was sipping beer from a bottle and smoking a cigarette.

"You boys got me trembling," he drawled. And he laughed and the men around him laughed.

There was no smile on David's face, only worry. He knew the men offering advice to him and to Dwaine owed favors and money to their father, Quinton Prichard. He knew also those same men were likely putting their wagers on Newell. He was glad his father was in Atlanta on a business trip. His father had threatened disinheritance if either he or Dwaine caused more trouble in Eden County, and he knew that his father would have been outraged over such behavior as the lard watermelon fight.

Dwaine flicked away his cigarette and one of the men ground it out with his shoe. "I never been to one of these things, but I sure don't want to hang around half the night waiting," he said in a loud, carrying voice. He paused, took another sip of beer. "David don't neither, do you, David?"

David shook his head. He glanced toward the water of the pond. "Maybe he won't show up," he mumbled.

"Oh, he'll show up," an old man with white hair and a sunken, toothless mouth said. He leaned in to Dwaine. "You never heard tell of Newell's Indian ways, has you?" he added.

"Him acting like he was Cochise?" Dwaine said. "Yeah, I heard them stories. Must of been a bigger fool than he is now."

The old man snickered. Spit sprayed from his mouth. "Not that," he said. "I'm talking about his ways in the water."

"What ways?" David asked suspiciously.

The old man stepped back and looked around him. "You'll see," he said in a whisper. "He's half beaver and half otter. You'll see." He turned and hobbled away.

A three-quarter moon rested like a bird's nest in the twig fingers of a beech tree that reached its outstretched arms above all other trees at Sorrow's Pond. The moon's light was a dull, washed-out gold over the flicker of lanterns and torches and campfires.

"What time is it?" Frank White asked Boggie Hazelhurst.

"Eight o'clock," answered Boggie.

"It's time," said Frank.

"It is," agreed Boggie.

And then, above the low rumbling of voices, a whippoorwill sang merrily from across the lake—loud, shrill, clear. The men suddenly stopped their talking and drinking. Lucky looked fearfully toward Ira and Ira calmed him with a nod. "Go get in the truck, Lucky," Ira said. "It's about to start."

The whippoorwill sang again, three times. The men moved quietly, respectively, to their staked-out places at the water's edge. They leaned toward the water, cupping their hands over their foreheads, staring into the canopy of darkness to the opposite side of the lake. The spill from the dull gold of the moon danced across the slick mirror of Sorrow's Pond, leaving light specks so tiny they had the look of shattered crystal.

"What's going on?" Dwaine asked in a demanding voice.

"Shut up, boy," Ira ordered sharply. He turned to Peavy Eaton. "Peavy," he said, "bring out the watermelon."

Peavy moved through the parting crowd, cradling a huge watermelon coated white with lard from the cooked fat of a slaughtered hog. He presented the melon to Ira and Ira inspected it attentively.

"Got the stem cut off," Ira mumbled. "Good, good." He rubbed a glob of lard over the nub where the stem had been, and then he wiped his hand across his shirt, leaving a lard streak. He nodded his approval. "Looks fine, Peavy," he said. "You done a good job."

"Got a truckload of them parked over there," Peavy said proudly. "Anybody wants one, they a quarter apiece. Bring half a dollar out in Atlanta."

Ira glared at him. "Peavy, I don't give one hoot in hell what you charging," he said in disgust. "Put it in the water."

Peavy ducked away and knelt at the water's edge and released the watermelon with a strong yet ceremonious shove. It rolled like a white fish and began to float toward the middle of the pond. No one spoke.

The whippoorwill sang out again, a sharp, single call.

The old man with white hair and sunken, toothless mouth began a gurgling whine in his throat. He did a little dance step, like a Pentecostal Holiness taken by the spirit.

"Boys," Ira said in a commanding voice to Dwaine and David, "get over here."

"What's going on?" Dwaine said again.

"Shut your trap," Ira growled. "Take them swimming trunks off and wait to I tell you when to go in."

"Naked?" Dwaine said.

Ira stepped close to Dwaine. "That's the way it's done, boy. It's the only rule they is. You do it naked. You don't like it, get your ass

35

out of here and keep on going, but you better remember one thing: won't nobody never let you forget it."

Dwaine looked around. Men were staring at him from dark faces.

"Suits me," he said. "But don't none of you boys faint when you see my pecker." He looked at David. "Com'on, David, let's get naked." He slipped out of his trucks and leaned over to pick up his knife.

"Put it down," Ira ordered.

Dwaine dropped the knife.

"Go stand by the water," Ira said.

Dwaine and David moved to the water's edge.

"It's getting close to the center," Boggie said, motioning toward the watermelon. The watermelon was floating slowly, turning in the water, gliding through the reflected light.

Ira called in a loud voice: "Newell."

The whippoorwill answered.

A wave of muttering swept the crowd in a chorus of oohs.

The Prichard twins looked across the water. Newell stood on a granite shelf on the water's edge. The dull spotlight of the three-quarter moon coated him. He was naked except for a full headdress of feathers. His arms were stretched high with opened palms. Claude Marks, a black man who worked with Newell on the sanitation truck, stood in the shadows behind him.

Dwaine cackled a loud laugh.

Across the water, Newell began to sway and chant.

"Aaaaaaaaaahyaaaaaaah...aaayeeeeeeyaaaaaaeee...."

The crowd was transfixed, watching Newell as though watching a mortal become a myth.

"What you doing, Tonto?" Dwaine called across the water. "Or are you Gee-ron-nee-mo?" He laughed hysterically and looked around for approval from the crowd. No one moved. No one spoke.

Newell answered: *"Aaaaaaaaahyaaaaaaaaahyaaaaa . . ."*

The old man with white hair and sunken, toothless mouth rubbed drool away from his chin. His body began to jerk.

Suddenly, Newell cried, *"Eeeeeeiiiiiiiyaaaaaa!"* He lifted the headdress of feathers and held it high, like an offering to the gods of the night, and then he turned slowly and handed the headdress to Claude.

"Hey, Claude, you better watch out," Dwaine called. "That looks like a buzzard you holding."

Newell's body stiffened. He raised one hand in the direction of the Prichard twins and then he spoke in a voice that carried across the lake, yet seemed like a whisper: "Boys, you can quit now if you want to. Won't nobody say nothing about it. You wade out in that water, they ain't no turning back. It'll just be me and you."

"Kiss our ass, Trashman," Dwaine yodeled. "You gonna be spitting up frog turds when they drag you out. You ain't much of a Indian, no how. I heard tell you come from some half-assed tribe called the Semi-holes." He laughed and turned to David. "Ain't that right, David?"

David did not speak. He did not laugh. He did not move.

Newell crossed his arms over his chest. He stood as erect as a statue on a town square. Across the lake, in the moon's light, he did not look fifty years old.

"Listen to me, boys," he called. "You never done this and I never been beat at it." He paused. "But I never been up against boys before—just men. Makes me feel a little sorry for you."

A few of the on-lookers laughed and Dwaine took a step forward, toward the lake. His mouth was twisted in anger.

"Where you going?" snapped Ira. "I'm the judge here. I tell you when to go."

Dwaine stepped back. "Get to it, old man," he snarled.

Ira moved to the edge of the water, to the spot reserved for the presiding judge. He carried a paper cup of mountain whiskey and a lantern.

"What's it look like, Ira?" a voice asked.

Ira lifted his lantern and studied the floating watermelon. It was center pond. "Looks about right," he announced. He turned to the Prichard twins. "You boys ready?" he asked.

"You wasting time, you waiting for us," Dwaine said in a loud, bold voice.

Ira turned toward Newell. He called, "What about you, Newell?"

"Anytime," Newell replied calmly.

"All right, let's get this straight," Ira commanded. "First one that gets that watermelon on shore, is the winner, and the Devil hang hell on what happens on the way."

A chorus of voices bellowed approval.

Ira raised his hand for attention. "Before we get started, let's have a round of applause for Peavy Eaton, who come up with the watermelon and the lard," he said.

A wave of applause flew up from the crowd. "Way to go, Peavy," someone shouted.

Peavy circled his hand over his head.

"All right," Ira announced to the men around him, "let's have at it." He raised his lantern. "On your mark…"

Dwaine leaned at the waist, like a sprinter in a race. David did a short step backward.

"Get set…" Ira called.

Dwaine began to move forward.

"Go!" Ira commanded.

A yell exploded in harmony from the crowd as Dwaine dove into the water and began to swim in strong strokes toward the watermelon. David followed cautiously.

Newell watched from his rock. He knew Dwaine and David were spending great energy absorbing the first shock of cold water. He had been swimming upstream for an hour before appearing on the bank, letting the chill seep into his body. He knew the waters of Asa's Spring. He had spent the summers of his childhood playing in its slow, cold current.

"Newell, you damn fool, get going!"

The command was from Ira, who had bet one hundred dollars on Newell.

Newell took three running steps and cannon-balled into the water like a thunderclap.

"Goda'mighty," exclaimed Boggie. "He must of knocked his pecker off."

"He likes to make a splash," said Ira.

Newell stroked twice with his arms, slithering across the top of the water. Then he kicked, ducked his head, and disappeared.

"He's gone under," someone shouted joyfully.

"Watch out, boys," another voice advised.

The old man with white hair and sunken, toothless mouth was at the water's edge, on his knees, clapping childishly. He squealed, "He's coming, boys."

The lard-coated watermelon began to bob crazily on the churning water. Dwaine was five feet from it. He kicked hard with his legs and lunged, catching it in his arms like a football. The watermelon popped from his grasp and skimmed past his shoulder and slid down his back. He muttered, "Damn." He turned in the water to look for David. David was fifteen feet away from him, treading water. "Get after it," he shouted.

And then the water suddenly parted beside Dwaine and Newell's shimmering body rose like a dolphin. With one leg, he kicked Dwaine in the pit of his stomach and Dwaine rolled away, folding his body with the pain. The watermelon was at Newell's face. He turned to find David, who was still treading water, his face wearing an expression of horror. Newell smiled. "Hey, David," he called. "You want it, boy?" He tapped the watermelon lightly with his fingers, guiding it toward David.

A shout exploded from the shore: "Watch out, Newell."

The warning came too late. Newell turned in the water as Dwaine's fist crashed down on his neck. His brain sputtered with hot lights and his head slapped against the surface of the water. Dwaine was over him, kicking hard, riding him by the shoulders, pushing him under.

For a moment, Newell was surprised by Dwaine's strength and he struggled to free himself. He turned his head to the surface and sucked a fresh wave of air into his lungs. Dwaine's fist caught him again, over his right ear, and Newell doubled into a knot, pulling his knees into his chest. He ducked his head and sank like a stone.

"He's gone under," Boggie said from the shore. "It's about to be over with."

Sinking had always been Newell's secret in lard watermelon competition. Unlike most men, he was not a natural floater; he was a natural sinker, and he had learned the advantage of fighting from the bottom of the water, preserving his strength by disappearing like a beaver and holding his breath like a man with spare lungs.

Dwaine thrashed at the water, hitting it with his fist, feeling for Newell, but Newell had dropped below him. He pushed from the spot with a scissors kick, guarding the top of the water with clenched fists. A few feet away, the watermelon floated gently toward David.

"Push it to the bank," Dwaine ordered. "Get behind it and push it. Don't try to grab it. Just push."

David paddled toward the watermelon. He slapped at it and missed. He stroked once with his arm, pulling into a glide.

"You got it, boy," a voice cheered from the shore. "Push it."

"Son of a bitch," another voice said, pronouncing each word with a sad drawl. "Looks like Newell's been had. Ain't nobody can stay down that long."

"You don't know Newell," argued Boggie. "He's got Indian lungs."

Under water, Newell's Indian lungs burned. His eyes felt as though they would rupture. Above him, David was in control of the watermelon, tapping it lightly, playfully, like a child with a toy sailing ship. The watermelon rolled closer to the bank, fifteen feet away.

"Hit it good, boy," someone urged gleefully.

"You got it, now," another voice judged.

David laughed aloud. The game he had feared was now child's play. He raised his free hand in a victor's salute. "Here it comes," he shouted.

And then David's body began to rise from the water, his arms clawing the air for balance, his shoulders twisting spastically as Newell exploded to the surface, pushing him upward.

A roar from the crowd of onlookers rolled around Sorrow's Pond.

"Goda'mighty," Boggie whispered in awe, "Newell throwed him clean out of the water."

Newell was on the surface, sucking air, fighting the unconsciousness swirling in his head. He made a great gulping sound and flicked his head, sending a spray of water from his hair.

"Get it, Newell," Boggie yelled.

"Bust it open," another voice added.

Newell's eyes cleared. To his left, he saw Dwaine struggling to hold David above the water.

And then the swimmers became still, staring at one another across the water like alligators on Florida lakes. The cheering stopped. The watermelon floated behind Newell's head.

"Boys," Newell said easily, "I'm coming after you." He smiled and sank slowly from sight, his hands cupped above his head. A curl of bubbles swirled from his disappearing fingers.

"You get the watermelon," Dwaine instructed David. "I'm going after him." He kicked backward, rolled on his side and slid smoothly beneath the surface.

"You better watch out," a voice shouted from the shore. "He's got them Indian lungs."

David stroked in a backward motion. His face searched the water fugitively. He could feel the cold stream of the main channel and he knew he was in the deepest spot of the lake. Something touched his foot—lightly, a sliding-over touch. A fish, he thought. He stroked hard with his right arm, pulling back. Again, something was against his foot, rougher than before, something sharp, like the fin of a catfish. He remembered what he and Dwaine had been told about Newell's fingernails. He heard the warning: *". . . they's like hooks."*

Ten feet away, Dwaine popped up from beneath the water. He lifted a large rock above his head.

"He's still under," David called, "and I'm getting out." He rolled on his stomach and stroked once with his left arm, and then he vanished, his body yanked from the top of the water as though he had fallen into a hole.

"Goda'mighty," shouted Boggie. "Newell's got him."

The water boiled with a storm of deep struggle and then David erupted to the surface beside Dwaine, bobbing like a mirrored reflection of his brother.

Dwaine raised the rock above his head. "Where is he?" he demanded.

David coughed water from his lungs. A look of terror covered his face.

On the shore, a murmur of awe became a babble of voices:

"Good Lord!"

"Where'd he go?"

"They's nobody can hold his breath that long, not even Newell."

Then Newell rose, as though on cue, silently breaking the water's surface like a periscope on a submarine. He was behind Dwaine and David and they did not see him. He reached across Dwaine's shoulder and plucked the rock from Dwaine's hand. Dwaine flailed clumsily in the water.

"You lose something?" Newell asked calmly. He held the rock up and made a fake, striking motion toward Dwaine's head. Dwaine flinched.

A chorus of laughter broke out on the shore.

Newell dropped the rock into the water. "Last time somebody tried to use a rock on me, he come near to drowning," he said. "I'm guessing you weren't thinking to hit me with it, though, was you? I'm guessing you was just trying to clean out the bottom of the lake."

David began to swim away, toward the shore. Dwaine paddled cautiously away from Newell's reach. He shouted, "David, get back here."

David did not stop his frantic swimming.

"He's gone," Newell said. "It's just me and you, boy. Better get you a mouthful of air. Me and you, we going under."

Newell's body rose from the water like an uncoiling snake. He fell across Dwaine, his left arm folding around Dwaine's neck, and the two dropped from sight.

A hoot of delight flew up from the shore of Sorrow's Pond.

Underwater, Newell tightened his grip on Dwaine. He was at the bottom of the lake, on its slick silt flooring, and he had Dwaine's face aimed like a shovel, plowing into the silt and clay. Then he released Dwaine and pushed him to the surface.

Dwaine's hair and face were covered with slime. He was swallowing desperately, rolling in the water like a broken ship.

Newell caught him by his hair and swam to shore in a lazy sidestroke. "Take him," he said to Boggie.

Boggie caught Dwaine by the leg and pulled him out of the water.

"Where's David?" Newell asked.

"Last I seen him, he was hiding over there behind a tree," Boggie said, "crying like a baby. You ought to be ashamed of yourself, picking on little boys like that." He laughed again.

"You still got to get that watermelon out of the water," Ira called.

"I'm about to do that," Newell said. "Fact is, I'm about to show you something you never seen."

The watermelon floated near the center of the dam. Newell pushed away from the shore and pulled easily in four long sidestrokes toward it.

"All yours," Ira pronounced in his voice of judgment. He held his lantern high. "All you got to do is get it out before them boys decide to jump back in."

"Well, good Lord, Ira, that could take a year or longer," Peavy said. "We ain't got that much time."

Laughter rose and rippled.

"All right, boys, now you about to see how Indians used to do it," Newell announced. He raised his hands above his head. His hands were spread, his fingers curled. He cried, "Aaaaaaaaaiiiiiieeeeee-yyyyaaa!" And then he jammed his fingernails hard against the watermelon, spearing it. He lifted it slowly from the water and held it above his head as the men crowding the banks of Sorrow's Pond bellowed in approval.

"Damn," whispered Ira in admiration.

Newell kicked gracefully in the water, swimming with his legs, until he reached the bank of the pond. He was still holding the watermelon above his head when he stepped out of the water and paraded triumphantly to where Dwaine was stretched across the grass.

He stood over Dwaine, smiling. "Told you, didn't I?" he said. He held the watermelon over Dwaine's head, then turned his wrists and dropped it. The watermelon exploded three inches from Dwaine's face, spewing him with juice.

"It's over," Newell proclaimed. He stepped back. "Somebody get their clothes so they can go home," he added. "Like I said, it's over."

Newell was wrong. Only the lard watermelon fight was over. The partying—the serious partying—had just begun. Claude Marks appeared from the opposite side of the pond with towels and Newell's clothes and feathered headdress, and Newell dressed himself with exaggerated ceremony, letting the feathers fall over his shoulders. Around him, the crowd yodeled and cheered and toasted him with beer and moonshine.

"You shouldn't of quit drinking, Newell," Boggie said. "Every man out here wants to buy you one."

"I made a pledge, Boggie," Newell replied. "Besides, I feel too good to mess it up, and since this is my last time for a lard watermelon fight, I want to remember it."

"You really retiring this time?" asked Ira.

"Enough's enough," Newell said.

And then, near Ira's truck, there was a bellowing cry of anger, and from the bed of the truck, Lucky shouted, "Mr. Newell! Mr. Newell!"

Newell whirled instinctively to his right and crouched, a cat's move. He saw Dwaine creeping toward him, holding his knife in his right hand.

"Put it down," Newell ordered evenly.

"Kiss my ass," Dwaine hissed. He lunged at Newell, swinging the knife.

Newell sidestepped the lunge like a matador teasing a bull. He crossed his hands at his waist and slapped at the silver buckle of his wide belt. It was a move no one at Sorrow's Pond had ever seen, and those who did see it would forever debate what happened in the blur of motion. They knew only that Newell was suddenly holding his belt in his right hand, twirling it, the silver buckle glittering in the light of moon and stars and lanterns and campfires.

In the years to follow, men would tell stories of how Dwaine made another lunge at Newell and how Newell's belt buckle cracked like a whip over Dwaine's knife-hand, forcing him to scream in pain and to drop the knife. "Like Lash LaRue," the men would proclaim in admiration.

They would chortle with remembered glee over the look of horror on Dwaine's face and they would tell how he turned to run, but was stopped by the crowd and thrown to the ground—each man claiming to have had a part in the stopping and throwing—and how Dwaine had rolled into a ball as Newell moved over him, twirling his belt.

They would describe in detail—the detail changing with each telling—how Newell picked up the knife and squatted before Dwaine and caught him by his long hair and in one swift motion, cut the hair at the scalp. And how Newell rose to his feet, hoisting the hair high, doing a little jitterbug-type dance and singing out his Indian war song—"Aaaaaaaaaaaaiiiiiiiiiieeeeeeeeeiiiii…"

"Damnedest thing you ever heard," was the way the men at Sorrow's Pond would describe it. "Make your skin crawl with that Indian yell of his."

Years later, the men who claimed to have been at Sorrow's Pond on the night of the last world's heavyweight lard watermelon fight, would gather at the funeral for Newell Proudfoot and they would again tell the tale of the scalping of Dwaine Prichard. Over and over, they would tell it.

And each telling would end with the words that make legends.

They would say of Newell: "He was something else, that boy was."

Felton Eugene Weaver
Becomes Famous

The Story of
Felton Eugene Weaver

Felton Eugene Weaver's resume advertised that he had been an acting student at the University of Georgia and had performed major roles in a dozen reputable plays for small, yet artistic theaters in New York City.

His physical appearance was given as tall (six-one), slender (175) and handsome (smoky brown eyes, a slight chin dimple, good teeth). His age was listed as twenty-eight. His record of citizenship noted that Felton had served with distinction during the Philippine campaign in World War Two.

The photograph stapled to Felton's resume had him posed in a pea jacket, collar upturned, a burning cigarette dangling at a tilt from his lips, his eyes squinting from the smoke. The photograph was purposely blurred to leave an impression of a steel-tough man—a Bogart leering at a Bacall.

The resume was a Hollywood lie.

Felton Eugene Weaver of Cuttercane, Georgia, had never been on campus at the University of Georgia.

He had never been in a play. In fact, he had never seen one.

He was five-ten. A beer band of flab ballooned over his belt, pushing his weight to 200. His eyes were brown, but shifty, not smoky. The slight chin dimple was a scar from a fight. His teeth were crooked and tobacco-stained.

He was thirty years old.

His military record was a blight on American honor.

Yet, none of the exaggerations—the deceptions—mattered to Felton. He wanted to be an actor, a movie star. He wanted to be remembered. He wanted to be a Somebody. Besides, he lived in Hollywood, California. In Hollywood, California, a lie was a temporary truth dressed in the finery of words.

Among Felton's most outrageous claims was a boast to his family in Cuttercane that he expected to be cast in a major motion picture in the near future, likely co-starring Betty Grable or Veronica Lake.

"My agent tells me it's in the bag," said Felton.

"Oh, honey, that's wonderful," said his mother, whose name was Clara.

"You lying, Felton," said his older brother, Rabe. "You never even seen Betty Grable."

"I damn sure have," countered Felton. "I been to her house a couple of times."

Rabe hooted a laugh. "Great God, boy, you something, you know that? I'm glad our daddy's not around to hear you lying like this. You come home once every five years or so and you not changed a lick. Not one."

"Don't talk that way to your brother," said Clara. "Maybe he has been to her house. You don't know."

"I been there," declared Felton in an irritated voice. "She's got a big place. One of these days, I'll get me a house just like it."

Rabe cackled. He clapped his hands once.

"I think that's nice, honey," his mother purred. "Maybe you'll let me come see you in a big house like that."

"Mama, you can come live with me," Felton promised. "Just as soon as I get my first big role, you can come out and live with me."

"What about me, Felton?" Rabe said sarcastically. "You gonna let me come out and live with you? Maybe I can meet me some of them Hollywood women you always talking about."

Felton stared haughtily at his brother. "You can come out and be my butler," he said. "Every big star needs him a butler."

Rabe glared hatefully. He said, "Yes sir, boy, you something, you know that? You got Mama eating out of your hand like you a big deal when you don't got so much as a slop jar to pee in."

"Leave him along, Rabe," warned Clara. "You saw his picture. Looks just like Clark Gable or Tyrone Power. How many pictures did you bring home for your mama, honey?"

"Thirty, Mama," Felton said gently. "I suspect they'll be some people around here wanting one when I get to be a star and I know they'll be hounding you."

"You gonna sign one of them for your mama, honey?"

"Mama, I'll sign all of them before I leave," Felton assured her. "That's what people do out in Hollywood. Sign a bunch of pictures ahead of time."

"You better go lay down naked in Asa's Spring if you think you gonna be in picture shows," Rabe said. "You're gonna need all the help you can get."

"Maybe I will," Felton said thoughtfully. "I took me a dip in it before I went off to the army and I come back without a scratch on me. Maybe that's what I need. Maybe I ought to go out there and wade around."

"You ever take Betty Grable out?" teased Rabe.

"Couple of times," Felton answered arrogantly.

Felton was not lying about going to Betty Grable's home or escorting her. He was a limousine driver in Los Angeles and twice he had been directed to pick up and deliver Betty Grable to movie studios. Each time he had secretly fantasized about being her leading man. It was possible, he thought. All he really needed was a break, a stroke of luck, the intercession of a friend of a friend of a friend who knew someone in a position of power.

But even Felton knew the odds were against him. It had nothing to do with his dreams; it had everything to do with his history.

As a young man in Cuttercane, Felton enjoyed the reputation of being a born driver of vehicles—any vehicle with a motor. He had a feather touch, dazzling reflexes, splendid vision ("Quick eyes," he bragged.), and he knew intuitively the limits of an engine. There were those who believed Felton could lay his hands on an ailing motor and cure it, as certainly as a revival preacher could cure boils and goiters.

When he was eighteen, Felton met a bootlegger from Knoxville, Tennessee, and the bootlegger hired him to run moonshine whiskey from east Tennessee to Raleigh and Durham in North Carolina. In 1940, the law caught Felton in a rundown and his lawyer bargained to exchange a year and a day on the chain gang for a tour of duty in the United States Army. He was at Pearl Harbor in 1941 when the Japanese attacked the naval base, but escaped injury by hiding in a church. A few months later he was in the Philippines as the driver for an army colonel and as a dealer in distilled whiskey for a civilian newspaper correspondent from Kentucky who operated a small still out of the basement of a hotel in Manila.

The Philippine Arrangement—a code name by the newspaper correspondent—was ingenious: whiskey-running to military encampments with an army colonel riding shotgun. Felton had devised a twenty-gallon carrying tank painted army brown that was welded to the back of the Jeep. He told the colonel it was for extra fuel and the colonel believed him.

"Sloshes a lot," the colonel said. "Makes me want to piss." The colonel had an infected prostate and had to urinate often.

"Made out of thin tin," Felton replied sadly. "Everything is nowadays." He added, "You let me know when you want to stop and I'll pull over."

The Philippine Arrangement ended on a side road late one afternoon when Felton stopped the Jeep to allow the colonel to urinate. A Japanese patrol stepped from the brush with fixed bayonets and one of them, an officer, ordered in a shrill, excited voice, "Up hands, cowboy." The colonel pissed on his pants.

The Japanese patrol forced Felton and the colonel to drive the Jeep into the forest to a small camp. In the interrogation that followed, the colonel gave his name, rank and serial number. Felton began negotiation with the Japanese officer, who had learned a kind of pig-English during a brief stay in Los Angeles to study filmmaking. Felton told the officer that he and his associate—the one impersonating an American colonel—had nothing to do with the war effort, but were keeping soldiers supplied with Philippine Kentucky bourbon, which he would be pleased to share with the Japanese officer as they discussed matters. The officer produced tiny clay cups and he and Felton began toasting one another, bowing with each swallow and jabbering in north Georgia drawl and pig-English Japanese.

The Japanese officer liked American cowboy movies and claimed he had once seen the great Randolph Scott on a street in Los Angeles. "Best cowboy of all cowboy," said the officer. Personally, Felton preferred Bob Steele over Randolph Scott, but he knew he was not in a position to argue. "Let's give a toast to old Randolph," said Felton, and they did. They toasted Randolph Scott and Bob Steele. They toasted Gene Autry and Roy Rogers and Johnny Mack Brown and Al "Lash" LaRue. They toasted Tokyo, Cuttercane, the colonel, Emperor Hirohito, American hotdogs and Japanese rice cakes. The Japanese officer spoke in lustful terms of beautiful women he had seen in Los Angeles and Felton became melancholy remembering a girl he had been living with in Pearl Harbor. They toasted Felton's sadness. They toasted one another for two hours and one gallon.

Later that night, Felton traded the Jeep with its twenty-gallon whiskey tank and two packages of Camel cigarettes for his freedom. The Japanese officer threw in the colonel and the tiny clay cups as a gesture of good will.

The colonel never reported the incident. A week after their safe return to Manila, Felton was back in Hawaii, where he remained the rest of the war, supervising the care and maintenance of cars for high-ranking government officials. He also operated a low-key, yet highly profitable blackmarket for rationed goods.

After the war, Felton took his war profits and, remembering the Japanese officer's description of beautiful women, went to Los Angeles, where he purchased a used limousine that Errol Flynn had once ridden in and he started Weaver's Hollywood Limousine Service. Three months later, the limousine threw a rod in rush hour traffic and Felton sold it for five hundred dollars. He then tried to teach a few Chinese laborers how to run a still, but the language barrier and Felton's impatience confused the laborers and they poured off the whiskey and kept the mash of his first run. Felton abandoned the still.

While working as a house painter, he met and married a girl from Kansas who had the personality and the hormones of a nymphomaniac. His wife persuaded him to open a whorehouse, employing the expertise and experience of a number of her friends. For a few months, Felton stayed dizzy counting the money that flowed in through the front and back door of the establishment. Still, he knew it was a risk and he was right. One night a minister from a Primitive Baptist Church led a revival-raid on the house and Felton's wife and her friends slipped out of the back door with their entire cash estate stuffed in a pillowcase while Felton pretended to repent under the red globe light on the front porch.

His war profits having dwindled to a few dollars, Felton returned to driving with the Star Wheels Limousine Service and soon earned the reputation of being the best driver in Los Angeles.

And that is where Felton met Sonny Paul Davis in 1951.

Sonny was from Nashville, Tennessee, the son of wealthy, indulgent parents. He had lived in Los Angeles for ten years, working first as a studio publicist and then advertising himself as an agent for the rush of hopeful young starlets who flooded Hollywood after the war. Sonny was handsome, articulate—a graduate of Vanderbilt University—and persuasive when he was not drinking. Regrettably, he drank often and when he did he often became a mutant: a slobbering, genetic throwback to the bootleggers of his ancestry.

Sonny liked Felton. Felton was a fellow Southerner. Felton did not judge him or belittle him because he had no clients actually registered with his agency. Sonny could call Star Wheels Limousine Service, ask for Felton and have Felton drive him around Beverly Hills for show. As they rode, he talked with Felton about his dreams of someday being a movie producer, or director. Occasionally, he invited Felton into an out-of-the-spotlight bar and they drank together. No one understood him as well as Felton when he was drinking. Felton had the only other authentic bootlegger's soul in Los Angeles.

It was on one of the nights when they were drinking that Sonny decided Felton should become an actor.

"I'm telling you, Felton, you could do it. I could be your agent," said Sonny in an excited voice.

"If I was to try it, you'd be my man," Felton declared.

"Well, hell's bells, let's do it," exclaimed Sonny. "It's happening all over. There's studios all over this place taking guys who didn't do diddley-squat before the war. I mean, truck drivers and bartenders and barbers. They're in the movies now. And you're a natural, Felton. You got just enough con in you to make it big."

"Don't it take more'n that, Sonny?" asked Felton.

"More?" Sonny replied. "Not out here. Con. That's the word. Look at all the movies. None of that stuff's real. It's just actors conning you into *thinking* it's real. And being at the right place at the right time is how it works. That's my job. That's what I do. I'm going to get you in the right places at the right time. All you got to do is be you. It's a hell of an angle, Felton. Chauffeur for the famous becoming famous, himself. From carting Terry Moore around to being in a love scene with her. You're going to be my start to the big time, Felton."

"I don't know," Felton protested. "I never been too good around big-time people. They always making me nervous when I have to drive them somewhere."

"They're just like you, Felton. Exactly. They're just people. That little rough edge you've got gives you an advantage, in fact. A lot like Bogart. That's the kind of picture we'll get of you. Like Bogart."

"I don't know, Sonny..."

"Well, by God, I do," Sonny roared. "That's been my trouble all along, Felton, and I just this minute realized it. I've been trying to find a starlet, some gorgeous broad with big tits, thinking that was the way to get started, but that's all wrong. All I ever do is wind up taking them to bed. What I need is somebody like Bogart, somebody with a rough edge, and you're it. You got rough edges all over you, Felton."

Felton was worried. "I don't know nothing about being no actor," he said. "Sometimes I guess I think about it, being out here, but I never done nothing like it."

"Don't worry about it," Sonny told him. "I'll write you a resume that'll make you look like you just arrived from the Old Vic in London. And we'll get a picture made tomorrow, and then we'll start work on what you need to do—like learning to speak properly and which silverware to use when you go out to some producer's house. This is going to work, Felton. I can feel it."

After Sonny presented him with the results of the photograph session, Felton became a believer. He was stunned by the face staring at him from behind the haze of cigarette smoke drifting across the picture. A shiver of pride shot through his chest.

"You right, Sonny," he said in a whisper. "I'm gonna be a movie star. By God, I am. I'm gonna call my mama tonight and tell her."

"Maybe we should change your name," Sonny suggested.

"What for?"

"Felton, everybody changes their name," answered Sonny. "You think Roy Rogers was named Roy Rogers? Hell, no. His real name is Leonard Slye."

Felton laughed. "Sonny, that's just a bald-faced lie. Roy Rogers is Roy Rogers."

"What it is now, but he used to be Leonard Slye," Sonny insisted. "He changed it when he got in the movies. And he's not the only one. Can you tell me what Hedy Lamarr's real name is?"

Felton stared at Sonny in shock. He shook his head.

"It was—get this, Felton—it was Hedwig Kiesler. And you know that new guy—Tab Hunter? You think anybody would name their son Tab? No way. His real name is Art Gelien. Think about that, Felton: Art Gelien."

"What do you think I ought to change my name to, Sonny?" Felton asked eagerly.

"I don't know," Sonny replied. "How about Biff?"

"Biff?" exclaimed Felton. "I'll whip your ass, you ever call me Biff."

"All right, how about Kip?"

"You pushing it, Sonny."

"Darrel. I like Darrel," Sonny said quickly. "Darrel Weaver."

"I knew a Darrel back home," Felton said. "He was a stuck-up little bastard."

"You got any ideas?" asked Sonny.

"Yeah," Felton said. "Felton. I like Felton. It was my grand-daddy's name, and far as I know there's nobody out here named Felton."

"We'll leave it Felton, then," agreed Sonny. "Of course, when you get a big role the director might want you to change it."

"Just so it ain't Biff or Darrel," Felton said.

Felton's first audition was for a western starring John Wayne, whose real name was Marion Michael Morrison, a revelation that almost caused Felton to leave California. No man should be called Marion, he said to Sonny.

The role did not have dialogue, explained Sonny, but it would provide necessary exposure for Felton.

"What I got to do?" asked Felton.

"Ride a horse," Sonny said. "Not much on-camera time, but it's important. There's a trail gang riding into town, just before the big showdown scene. They ride in, get off their horses, and go into a saloon."

The horse threw Felton three times and Felton was fired.

"A horse," Felton said to Sonny, "is one of God's dumbest animals. If it had been a mule, I could have done it."

"Maybe we better forget about westerns," Sonny suggested. "They tend to have horses in them."

A month later, Felton was hired for a crowd scene in a movie about Roman gladiators. He was fired for accidentally jabbing one of the supporting actors with a spear.

"You'd think the son of a bitch could take a little jab," Felton complained bitterly.

"In the nuts?" Sonny wailed in exasperation.

Felton's next role was as a dead body in a detective story. He couldn't keep his eyes from fluttering and was dismissed.

"It was them lights," Felton told Sonny. "They was too bright. I got quick eyes. They can't take much light. Seems to me they would have used dimmer lights on a dead body, anyhow."

"Maybe they should have used real bullets," snapped Sonny.

"I thought the blood looked real good, though," Felton said. "Looked like I was gushing, didn't it?"

Surprisingly, Felton's failures did not discourage Sonny; they angered him. He became determined to make Felton Eugene Weaver a movie star or spend his entire inheritance trying. It was more than a challenge; it was an obsession.

"We've got to start over," Sonny asserted. "Start from the ground up. We've got to have a plan."

"And I got to go home," Felton said. "It's my mama's birthday next week."

"What's the name of that place again?" asked Sonny.

"Cuttercane. It ain't much of a place, though," Felton told him.

"I like that name. Cuttercane," Sonny mused. "Maybe we should call you Felton Cuttercane."

"Good God, Sonny," Felton said in astonishment.

"All right, all right," Sonny mumbled. "When you get back, I'll be ready. I'll have a plan."

When Felton returned from Cuttercane, with the echo of his brother's torment still playing in his memory, he was met by Sonny at the Los Angeles airport.

Sonny had a plan.

"I've been working my ass off," Sonny declared proudly. "Haven't had a drink, Felton. Not one. Not a drop. You are about to become a class-A, five-pointed, Oscar-grade movie star with gold glitter, but you've got to do exactly what I say."

Felton could hear his brother's hyena laugh. He could see the soft smile of his believing mother. He remembered his dip in Asa's Spring on the day before leaving to return to Los Angeles. He said to Sonny, "You got my word on it. What're we gonna do?"

"You're going into training, Felton. That's what's been missing: training. Tomorrow you're going to meet Ursula."

"Who?"

"Ursula Bernhard. She's a teacher."

"What kind of teacher?"

"An acting teacher, Felton. She's the damnedest woman I've ever met. Word is, she taught Marlene Dietrich how to act, but she won't say. I asked her straight out. All she did was smile."

"I don't know, Sonny," Felton said hesitantly. "I never was much good in school."

"It's not school," Sonny explained. "My God, is that what you think? It's private tutoring. Ursula's going to work just with you. She's going to get those rough edges shined up a little bit."

"What's that mean?"

"Teach you how to talk proper," Sonny said. "Teach you how to stand like an actor, walk like an actor, think like an actor." He tapped his temple with his finger. "Think," he added emphatically. "That's what's missing, Felton. You've got to learn to *think* like an actor. Ursula will help you do that."

The first session with Ursula Bernhard was the following morning. She stood regally before Felton, glaring at him. She had disgust in her eyes.

"He ist a slob," she said suddenly, loudly.

"But Ursula—" Sonny began.

Ursula stopped him with a sweep of her hand.

"Look at him," she snapped. The accent of her voice was like the swiping blade of a knife. Felton slumped. The color drained from his face.

"Stand up, slob," she growled.

Felton snapped to a remembered military posture. Ursula smiled triumphantly.

"Ist better," she said. She circled him slowly, her eyes squinting, her nostrils flared as though offended. She began to shake her head sadly. She clucked her tongue. "He," she declared at last, "ist the most ugly man I have ever seen. You want me to make of him an actor?"

62

"They're going for the natural look these days," Sonny said weakly.

Ursula whirled toward Sonny. "Natural?" she sneered, saying the word in three distinct syllables. "Then get me natural man. This man ist a slob. Slobs cannot be actors."

"Now wait just a damn minute," Felton said angrily. "I'm standing here, I'll have you know."

Ursula laughed, a rolling, robust laugh. She clapped her hands. "What ist that?" she said. "The grunting of a swine, maybe?"

Sonny stepped forward, close to Ursula. He said in a quiet manner, "That, Ursula, is the sound of money. You see, old girl, I'm worth a few million and I say you teach my friend here how to act, and I say he looks one hell of a lot like John Barrymore. You agree and I double your fee."

Ursula's eyes narrowed again. She lifted her chin, turned her eyes seductively to Felton and smiled sweetly. "Maybe is the light," she said. "Come, young man, step close to Ursula."

Felton moved one step. He looked at Sonny. Sonny winked.

"Ah, yes," Ursula said. "There ist a certain—charm. Maybe we can do something here, yes?"

"That's better," said Sonny. "Let's get started."

For six months, Ursula raged and Felton quaked.

She forced him to walk with the image of holding a silver dollar between his buttocks. She placed pebbles under his tongue (Felton swallowed two of them) and demanded that he recite nursery rimes while standing on one foot. She insisted he study ballroom dancing with a girl who had an eerie resemblance to his vanished wife, and she enrolled him in a fencing class with a skinny Spainard who blew kisses from behind his steel-meshed mask. She taught him to sit in a chair without looking at it, a trick of touching the edge of the seat with the calf of his leg. She drilled him on counter turns and open stances and pivots. She dispatched him to a hair stylist and had his hair dyed wheat blonde. She ordered him into a girdle to redistribute his beer band. She had his teeth capped.

At the end of the six months, Ursula delivered to Sonny a dazed, but redone, Felton Eugene Weaver.

Sonny was impressed.

"My God, Felton, you almost look real," Sonny said in awe. "You deserve a celebration. Name it, boy, and it's on me."

"I want to see that fencing fellow," Felton told him in a remarkably strong voice.

"Why?" asked Sonny.

"I'm gonna whip his ass," Felton declared.

"You can do that later," Sonny said. "You come with me. I've got a surprise for you."

The surprise was a ride to the Beverly Hills Hotel and the Polo Lounge as a passenger in a Star Wheels Limousine. The Star Wheels driver, who was named Carey Murphy, did not recognize Felton.

"You're a new man," Sonny whispered in the back seat. "What did I tell you?"

"I can't believe it," Felton whispered in reply. "I was working with Carey for five years and he don't know who I am."

"Doesn't know," corrected Sonny.

"Yeah."

"We'll tell him later," Sonny said.

"He'll get a kick out of that," Felton predicted.

In the Polo Lounge, Sonny ordered a bottle of champagne and cigars and quietly directed Felton's attention to the movie stars who wandered in and out of the room. Felton was speechless.

"This is the place to be seen," Sonny said. "Anybody who's worth a damn shows up here. Someday, they'll be pointing at you and they'll be saying, 'There's Felton Weaver.' That's what they'll be saying. You can count on it."

A page in a starched uniform and a bowl cap moved through the lounge, calling, "Paging Miss Gloria Swanson, paging Miss Gloria Swanson." He looked exactly like the page in the Philip Morris cigarette commercials.

Felton stared in amazement. He asked, "She here, Sonny?"

"Maybe," Sonny said. "Maybe not. It's just good public relations. And in case you're wondering, her real name is Gloria May Josephine Svensson."

Another page sang out, "Paging Milton Berle, paging Milton Berle."

Felton whistled softly.

"That'd be Mendel Berlinger if you used his real name," said Sonny. He stood. "I'll be back in a minute," he added.

"Where you going, Sonny?" Felton asked.

"To take a leak. You sit right here. Have some more champagne," Sonny said. He laughed, wagged the cigar in his mouth and walked away. He returned in five minutes.

"Now, my man, we are about to make you known," Sonny announced.

"How?" asked Felton.

"Don't worry about it. Trust me."

A third page, looking exactly like the other two pages, wandered among the tables holding a slip of paper that was cupped in the palm of his hand. He looked at it quizzically, then began his singsong: "Paging Felton Weaver, paging Felton Weaver."

Sonny cackled and slapped Felton on the back.

"Damn," Felton whispered. He blinked his eyes rapidly and swallowed hard.

"What's the matter?" asked Sonny. "You look like you're about to cry."

"I wish my mama could of heard that," Felton said.

Felton's first actual role as an actor occurred two weeks later in a gangster movie. In it, Felton played an innocent bystander in a bank robbery. He had one line: "Don't shoot me, please." He did it in four takes. That night he called his mother and told her he had finally become an actor. "I'm on my way, Mama," he said. His mother wept and Felton wept. She said to him, "Better send me some more pictures, honey. They'll be people knocking my door down when they hear you're a movie star."

The scene was cut from the movie.

"That's it," Sonny stormed. "Now, I'm pissed, I mean really pissed. I'm tired of this one-horse town. They wouldn't know talent if it kicked them in the gonads."

"Maybe I better go back to driving the limo," Felton suggested heavily.

"No, you're not," bellowed Sonny. "I'm not giving up. I told you, I'm pissed and when a Davis gets pissed things get ugly. I'm ready to do something drastic."

"Like what?"

Sonny paced and stroked his face with his hands. He was deep in thought. "What's the greatest movie ever made?" he asked.

"I like that one about Jim Thorpe," Felton said. "It just come out, but I've been to see it three times already."

Sonny stared at Felton in disbelief. "Felton, it can't hold a candle to *Gone With the Wind*," he said. "The greatest movie ever made was *Gone With the Wind*."

"Yeah, I liked that one," admitted Felton.

Sonny began to pace again. "And what was it about?" he said dramatically.

"That sonofabitch Yankee burning Atlanta," Felton declared. "Sherman."

"Well, that was part of it," Sonny conceded, "but it was more about the ravages of the Civil War, and that's the answer."

"To what?" asked Felton.

Sonny walked to the window of his apartment and parted the curtain with his hand. In the distance, he could see the lights of Hollywood. He said, "What we're going to do, Felton, is make our own movie about the Civil War. It'll make *Gone With the Wind* look like a wiener roast on a church picnic." He dropped the curtain and turned back to Felton. There was a smug expression on his face. "I'm rich," he added. "At least my daddy is. I'll pay for the damn thing myself. I'll produce it. I'll direct it." He took two steps toward Felton. "And you, Felton, you'll star in it."

Sonny Paul Davis was inspired, more inspired that he had ever been, and it surprised him. He had heard people speak of desire that blazed like an unquenchable fire in their souls, but he had never known such a moment. His parents were wealthy. They funneled money to him as a matter of obligation and as a habit of extravagance. If Sonny wanted anything, he purchased it. Money had been the salve of healing for his restlessness and it had also been the narcotic that dulled his vision. Now he had both inspiration and a clear vision. The blaze in his soul ignited in his chest, in his brain, in his mouth, and its heat became an aura around him. Sonny had more than a scheme; he had a mission.

He called his father in Nashville and described his plan: a new motion picture company to be called Davis and Davis Productions. His father would be chairman of the board while he, Sonny, would be president and executive producer. He assured his father there would be celebrities begging to become part of the action. "You'll be another Zanuck," he predicted. "Or Goldwyn or Mayer or Disney. We should have done this years ago."

His father reluctantly agreed to the proposition, though privately he did not believe Sonny would ever make a movie. To his father, Sonny was a dreamer with the business sense of a gnat and he had learned the hard way—through experience—not to expect anything more than grief from one of Sonny's schemes. Still, he pretended enthusiasm, knowing too well that Sonny was under the protection of his domineering wife, who believed her only son was sensitive and gifted, but a late bloomer.

"Just think things through before you do them," his father advised Sonny.

"I always do, Daddy," Sonny said.

The first thing Sonny did was hire a screenwriter named Gordon Peabody. Gordon had once written comedy sketches for Mack Sennett and, later, grade-B westerns for Republic Pictures. He had a reputation as a drunk and a has-been, but also as a man who wrote with blinding speed if the carrot of money was dangled before him.

Sonny explained what he wanted.

"Another *Gone With the Wind*? That's it?" Gordon said.

"That's it, but this time I want to see some heroic stuff from the Confederates. Beef it up a little," Sonny told him.

"I like that," Gordon said. "I can do it."

In their negotiation, Sonny agreed to rent for Gordon an expensive hotel suite stocked with expensive scotch and then to leave him alone for a month.

While Gordon was writing, Sonny began to put together a production crew. In the first week, he hired a line producer, a cinematographer, a sound engineer, a makeup artist, a set designer, a lighting director, an assistant director and a secretary. "We'll need a lot more people," he explained to Felton, "but we'll get them."

"When we gonna start shooting?" Felton asked anxiously.

"Soon as I get the script," Sonny told him. "Gordon's hard at work on it."

"How's he doing?"

"Don't know," Sonny confessed. "Haven't heard from him, but if I know Gordon, it's going all right." There was a furrow of worry on Sonny's face.

Gordon emerged, as he had promised, at the end of the month. He was exhausted. He had lost ten pounds. His eyes were bloodshot. His hands trembled. The scotch was gone. But he was exuberant.

"Here it is," he said triumphantly to Sonny. "It's a bloody masterpiece."

The script was fat and heavy. It had not been clean-typed and there were xed-out words blanketing the pages. The title read:

The Wind Blows Free

A screenplay

By Gordon Peabody

"Is that the title, or a joke?" Sonny asked.

"You said you wanted another *Gone With the Wind*," Gordon replied smugly, "but you wanted it to celebrate the South. Well, you got it. It makes that nonsense Margaret Mitchell wrote read like drivel."

Sonny was both excited and apprehensive. "What's it about?" he asked.

Gordon sipped from the scotch he had taken from Sonny's bar. He leaned his head against the pillow of the armchair and gazed thoughtfully at the ceiling. "It's a twist, Sonny," he said. "A movie breakthrough. In my story, the South wins the war and it's not Sherman who lights the torch, it's Robert E. Lee. He burns everything in sight, from Washington, D.C., to Canada. Scorches Sherman's ass in New York." The smile grew in his face. "You think burning

Atlanta was something, Sonny, wait until you see New York go up in flames."

"I don't know, Gordon," Sonny said hesitantly. "Sounds expensive."

Gordon shrugged his shoulders and yawned. "You didn't ask me to pay for it, just to write it. Do what you want with it. I'm going to bed and sleep for a week."

"Yeah, you do that, Gordon," Sonny said. "I'll let you know what I think."

Gordon Peabody's screenplay called for four thousand cast members and all the horses in Texas. It included the burning of Washington, Baltimore, Philadelphia, and New York. It featured the bloodletting of six major battles, the sinking of three warships off Long Island, and the use of crude bombs dropped from hotair balloons. The hero of the plot (Felton's role) was a Confederate patriot who was a pyromaniac and a lover of beautiful women.

The first page read:

FADE IN:

EXT. A BATTLEFIELD IN VAXXX VIRGINIA. MID-SUMMER, 1864. EARLY MORNING.

The SHOT PANS the batxxxtxx battlefield, showing two xxxthoxx thousand Confederate xxx soldiers awakening from sleep, beginning to xxxss stir in the earxxx early morning light. SOUND of horses, birds, low tgxxx talking.

SHOTS show men coxxx cooking breakfast, cleaning rifles, wrxs writing letters. All have tired look axs aboxx about them. They have been at war and it shows.

SHOT zeroes in on spsxx special tent, where GENERAL ROBERT
E. LEE sits at a maksxxx makeshift table. On the table is a mdxxx
model of a hotair balloon. The Genrxx General is studying it as
PRIVATE BEAU MAKEPEACE points to the balloon.

BEAU

We'll just load it up with my new firebombs, General, and then
we'll float overhead and drop them down. They'll brxxx burn like
the fired-up hsxxx hole of hell.

GENERAL LEE

(Admiringly)

Looks like the real thing, Private. Myxxx Maybe it'll help us make
the Yanks turn tail.

BEAU

(Proudly)

I promise it, sir. I've burned many a house and barn with this down
in Georgia.

GENERAL LEE

And what's it called, Pvxxx Private?

BEAU

Some call it a firebomb, sir, but I lkxxx like air bomb. It'll have them
Yankees running or my name's not Beau Makepeace.

ZOOM to CLOSEUP of the Gaxxx General. He has a pleased lkxxx
look on his face.

When he finished reading the script, Sonny was trembling. He whispered to himself, "Godalmighty, it'll take a billion dollars to do this thing. That sonofabitching Peabody, I'll kill him."

It took two days for Sonny to compose himself. He said to Felton, "We've got to do a little rewriting, make a few compromises, tweak it here and there. Things I can do myself."

"You?" said Felton.

"Me," answered Sonny, his voice filling with confidence.

Sonny's first compromise was to burn Gordon Peabody's script in his fireplace. He then sat at his typewriter and began to write.

In Sonny's story, the conflict was not between two armies, but a bastardly evil motorcycle gang and a lone, brave farm laborer named Bret Holley, who also rode a motorcycle and was in love with the farmer's daughter. It would be a perfect role for Felton, Sonny reasoned. It involved a motor and wheels.

Writing the script was surprisingly simple, Sonny discovered. He first made a list of every great movie scene he could remember, from cowboys pulling the bars off jailhouse windows with their horses to jousting matches between knights. When he finished he had twenty-six scenes. As he wrote, he checked them off, like checking off items on a grocery list.

In ten days, he was finished.

"Felton," he announced, "this is going to win an Academy Award."

"Sounds good," said Felton. "That'd make Mama happy."

"Wait'll you read the part about a jousting match on motorcycles, using switchblades," Sonny enthused. "It'll make your butt pucker. It'll be the greatest action sequence ever done. It'll make *The African Queen* look like a pleasure cruise on the Mississippi."

"Switchblades?" Felton said suspiciously.

"Don't worry," Sonny assured him. "We'll fake it. You won't get cut. The way we'll shoot it, you won't even have anybody around but you. We'll use a stuntman for the close-ups." He handed the script to Felton. "Come on, read the first couple of pages. Tell me what you think."

Felton read:

FADE IN:

EXT.   THE BACKYARD OF A LARGE FARM IN TENNESSEE, EARLY MARCH, 1953. DUSK.

A muscular, handsome man (BRET HOLLEY) is working diligently on an old motorcycle near the barn. He is oblivious to anything but the motorcycle. He listens intently as the motor spits, catches, runs. In the BACKGROUND a very pretty, sexy girl approaches. She is in the shaft of light from the setting sun. The sun makes her thin sundress appear translucent and the nakedness of her body—her round, globed breasts, her softly curving abdomen, the darkness of her hips—is easily seen. KAREN ARCHER, who is eighteen, but a woman, stands and watches Bret. When he turns off the motor and wipes his hands on the front of his shirt, she speaks. The SHOT covers the scene.

KAREN

(Sultrily)

Hello.

Bret is startled momentarily. He whirls, his fists ready, and looks at Karen. He sees her body against the sunlight.

BRET
(Embarrassed, shy)
Uh, hello, Miss Karen.

KAREN
Didn't see me, did you?

BRET
Uh, no'm.

KAREN
But you're sure looking at me now, aren't you, Bret?

BRET
(Averting his eyes)
Uh, yes'm. Uh, no'm.

Karen laughs and moves closer to Bret. She presses down her dress seductively with her hands.

KAREN
(Purring)
You're not going to start stuttering are you, Bret?

Bret pushes his hands in his pockets. He shakes his head slowly.

KAREN
And you're not going to start drooling, are you?

Bret toes the ground with his shoe. He shakes his head again.

KAREN

Well, that's good. I just came out to make sure you're going to be
here tonight. Daddy's got to be away and I'm all by myself and you
know how that awful motorcycle gang keeps after me. Will you
watch out for me tonight, Bret?

BRET

Yes—yes m'am.

KAREN

Don't go getting scared, Bret. If anything happens, you just need to
ride that old rickety motorcycle you got down to the sheriff's office.
And if you run into the Lone Biker on the way, you can send him
over and let him take me out of here. I'd love to ride on his gas
tank.

When Felton finished his reading, he handed the script back to
Sonny. There was a puzzled look on his face.

"You get it?" Sonny asked expectantly.

"Uh—"

"This guy, Bret Holley—that's you, Felton—and the Lone Biker
are one and the same," Sonny said. "It's like Clark Kent and
Superman or Bruce Wayne and Batman. This guy Bret fools around
with an old beat-up World War Two piece of junk, but in the back of
the barn, under some hay, he's got the biggest damn Harley-Davidson
known to man and he's got a black leather jacket with real silver doo-
dads all over it, and he wears a black mask, just like the Lone
Ranger."

Felton smiled. He liked the idea. He could see himself on a
Harley-Davidson in a black leather jacket, his eyes covered
dramatically with a mask. And his brother Rabe had said he'd never

amount to anything, he thought. Damn Rabe. Before long, Rabe would be singing a different tune.

"What happens?" Felton asked.

"Action, that's what happens," Sonny roared. "Action, action, and more action. This motorcycle gang from Knoxville keeps tormenting that poor little girl because the leader of the gang has the hots for her, but the Lone Biker is always there, just like Zorro."

"Yeah, I can see that," Felton said. He added, "But I never heard of motorcycle gangs. They got some in Knoxville?"

"Felton, who gives a damn?" Sonny replied. "It's a movie. Take the script and start memorizing it. We start shooting as soon as I line up the rest of the cast." He cackled a high laugh. "If they think *High Noon* was something, wait until they see *The Lone Biker.*" He turned to Felton. A large smile rested on his face. "Where do you think I'm going to have the world premiere, Felton?"

"Where?" Felton asked anxiously.

"In your hometown," Sonny answered. "Right there in Cuttercane."

"Sonny, we don't got a movie theater in Cuttercane," Felton said. "It's just a little bitty place."

"Where'd you go to see movies when you were growing up?" Sonny asked.

"Sometimes we'd go to Cleveland, or sometimes Hiawassee," Felton told him. "They got a lot of stores."

"Well, that's where we'll do it, then," Sonny announced. "We'll have the world premiere in one of those cities."

If Sonny had failed to write classical literature in *The Lone Biker,* he had succeeded in fashioning a role that did not terrify Felton. As Bret, the stumbling, suffering farm hand, all Felton had to do was mimic some of the farmers he had known from the Cuttercane Valley. As the Lone Biker, with a mask covering his eyes, he only had to remember the lessons of Ursula Bernhard, and to help with the transition, Sonny hired Ursula to be on location during the Lone Biker scenes, and under the whiplashes of her voice Felton assumed a persona that was semi-impressive. When he spoke as the Lone Biker, his voice was deep and precise. He stood erect, his shoulders squared. In his black leather jacket, he looked heroic. Still, to Ursula, he was an insult to the art of the cinema. She pronounced him a fool and demanded an increase in her fee.

The cast of *The Lone Biker* agreed with Ursula. They laughed openly at Felton. They ignored him. They treated him with Hollywood arrogance and disdain. Only the motorcycle gang—real bikers, not actors—respected him. Felton was the most spectacular bike rider any of them had ever seen and he spent his off-camera time with them, teaching tricks that were, to Felton, as natural as walking.

To Sonny's surprise and relief, Felton did not seem bothered by the treatment he received from Ursula and the cast. The only person who truly distracted him was Connie Denmark, who had been cast in the role of Karen Archer. Connie was beautiful. She had large, hazel eyes, full, plump lips, a voice that went through Felton like a soft wind. He had never seen a body as grand as Connie's, and he began to take morning and afternoon naps in search of the erotic dreams that visited his sleep at night. Still, in her presence he was helpless and their scenes together were forced and trite. "He's a jerk," Connie said to Sonny.

"Give it time," Sonny told her. "He just needs some experience."

"He needs a new life," Connie retorted.

The contentious disregard that Connie had for Felton made a dramatic improvement one morning when Sonny decided to shoot the movie's final scene while his line producer searched for a location to stage a square dance that had the bikers crashing the party.

"It's the way we shoot movies," Sonny explained to Felton. "We sort of jump around all over the place. I know of cases where they've done things almost backward—shooting the last scene first and the first scene last. It'll work. We'll just piece everything together."

The last scene of *The Lone Biker* was, for Sonny, tender and tragic. The Lone Biker is injured in his switchblade jousting match with the leader of the motorcycle gang and as he curls on the ground beside his fallen Harley-Davidson, Karen cradles him in her arms, weeping. She whispers that the leader of the motorcycle gang has fallen on his own knife and is dead, and then she gently removes his mask and discovers that the Lone Biker is, in reality, Bret Holley. She kisses him passionately, dedicating her love and her body to him. The Lone Biker rises painfully, pulling himself from her arms. He lifts his Harley-Davidson and, bleeding profusely, rides away as Karen wails and calls out, "Come back, Bret, come back. . . ."

"They'll be crying in the aisles," predicted Sonny.

The day the scene was scheduled to be shot, both Connie and Felton reported drunk to the set. Connie slurred to Sonny that being drunk was the only way to get through the scene with Felton and Felton admitted shamefully that being drunk was the only way he could overcome his fear of Connie.

"I don't believe this," Sonny moaned. "John Ford never had to deal with this. Do you think Alfred Hitchcock puts up with this kind of nonsense? Nobody does." He paraded angrily before the crew, pondering his options. Finally, he said in resignation, "All right, let's shoot the damn thing."

The scene was shot in one take. The crew applauded robustly when it was over. Ursula hugged Felton. "At last, here ist my actor," she cooed.

Sonny was shocked. He pulled Felton away and asked what had happened.

Felton smiled shyly. "Damned if I know," he said. "She was rubbing up against me like I was a piece of sandpaper and she had a belly itch and then she stuck her tongue halfway down my throat when we was kissing. I just let it happen."

"It looked hot," said Sonny. "I can tell you that. It looked hot."

"It was," Felton replied. "She said she wanted to have a drink with me later on tonight."

An expression of disbelief flashed across Sonny's face. "You old dog," he said. "You better hope she's still drunk."

That night, Felton made love to Connie Denmark for five hours. It was, he bragged to Sonny, the finest night of his life, even better than the parties he had attended in his ex-wife's whorehouse.

When the filming of *The Lone Biker* was completed, Felton left for Cuttercane to visit with his mother and brother and to preen before childhood friends, telling them exaggerated stories of his relationship with Connie Denmark. He had a photograph of himself and Connie in the passionate embrace of their love scene. His childhood friends were in awe. None of them had ever believed anything Felton told them.

"You are one lucky sonabitch," his friends said. "How'd you get so lucky, Felton?"

"Some things just happen the right way," Felton pontificated. "But maybe it weren't nothing I did," he added, winking knowingly. "Maybe it was Asa's Spring. I took a wade in it last time I was home."

His friends laughed. One of them said, "If I could get me a woman like Connie Denmark, I'd grow gills and live in that old mudhole."

The visit with his mother and brother was relaxing for Felton, but he had a yearning for Connie and he worried about Sonny. Sonny had not called as he promised he would.

"Maybe he's busy, honey," his mother suggested.

"Well, he said he'd be editing," Felton replied professionally. "I guess that's it. It's got to be ready in a couple of months for them Academy Awards people to look at it."

"Why don't you call him, honey?" his mother said.

"Maybe I will," Felton told her.

Sonny did not return Felton's calls. His secretary said that Sonny was working feverishly day and night and that his mood was not good.

"Tell him I'll be back soon," Felton said.

"Maybe you should stay a few more days," the secretary suggested. "He's really tied up."

When Felton returned to Los Angeles a week later, Sonny was jubilant. "It's done," he announced. "You're going to love it, Felton."

"When can I see it?" asked Felton.

"When everybody else does—on the night of the premiere," Sonny told him. "I've got the prints locked up and nobody's seeing them until I'm ready. I had to make a few changes here and there, shoot a couple of more scenes, but you'll love it, Felton. You're a star. They'll never forget you."

"What kind of changes, Sonny?" Felton wanted to know.

"Just—stuff," Sonny replied. "It's called doctoring, Felton. Everybody does it. When you finish shooting a movie you put it together and then you see if there's anything missing, something that might make it more appealing. I saw a few things, but it didn't involve shooting any more scenes with you, so I didn't call you." He smiled knowingly at Felton. "Don't worry, you still have your love scene with Connie. It's hot, like I said. And, by the way, don't go looking for her. She got married last week to that Italian director and he took her off to Rome."

80

The news of Connie's marriage was disappointing to Felton, but the news of the movie was pleasing. "I can't wait to see it," he said.

The poster advertising *The Lone Biker* was splashy and teasing. It was dominated by a bold drawing of the Lone Biker on his Harley-Davidson, with the front wheel high off the ground, like a horse pawing the air. A girl with the likeness of Connie Denmark was on the back of the motorcycle, clinging to the Lone Biker. She was wearing a flimsy dress with see-through qualities. Her breasts pushed forward, straining to tear through the fabric. Her hair flowed in the wind. Her face carried the expression of sexual exhilaration. A single, promising line was at the top of the poster in dark, block lettering: WHO IS THE LONE BIKER AND WHERE IS HE FROM? Below the picture was another line: THE TRUTH IS TOO SURPRISING TO TELL. SEE IT FOR YOURSELF.

Sonny had the poster framed for Felton and Felton mailed it to his mother. He included in the package another fifty photographs he had autographed. "You'll be needing these," he wrote.

A week before the premiere of *The Lone Biker* at the Silver Screen Movie Palace in Hiawassee, Sonny and Felton flew to Atlanta and rented a car and drove to Athens, which was eightyfive miles from Hiawassee, and the home of the University of Georgia.

"This is where we need to be staying," Sonny explained to Felton. "If we went to Hiawassee or Cuttercane, everybody would just be staring at you. In Athens, they'll be talking about you, and that's what matters. We'll get all these college kids fired up and they'll spread the word."

In Athens, Sonny rented a suite of rooms at a hotel and established a premiere headquarters. He stocked the rooms with whiskey and arranged press parties. The press appeared nightly to drink Sonny's whiskey and to eat from his abundant *hors d'oeuvres* trays. They interviewed Sonny and Felton. Felton wore his black leather jacket and posed for pictures on a borrowed Harley-Davidson. By the end of the week, the press had made celebrities of Sonny and Felton and *The Lone Biker* was being touted in Athens as a possible Academy Award nomination, though Sonny had stubbornly refused to let anyone see the movie. He would not, in fact, let anyone near the canisters that held the film.

Early on the day of the premiere, Sonny and Felton drove to Hiawassee and met with Oscar Barton, owner of the Silver Screen Movie Palace. Sonny was dressed in a white suit with a thin black tie. He looked exactly as Oscar believed a Hollywood producer-director-writer should look—creative. Felton was dressed as the Lone Biker, without the mask.

"You boys look good," Oscar told them. "You look like Hollywood."

Felton flexed the muscles in his arms. He lifted his chin theatrically. "Thought maybe some of the people would like to see what I was wearing in the movie," he said.

"That's good, Felton, that's good," Oscar enthused. "It's the biggest thing that's ever happened in Hiawassee, and that's the truth. We've got everything ready."

Oscar had closed the theater for two days and had hired a dozen high school students to clean and paint it. "Even scraped the chewing gum off the bottom of the seats," he announced proudly. "Smell that paint, Felton. You ever smell anything that clean? It's cleaner than the hospital. You could take out somebody's appendix on the popcorn machine."

"Smells clean, all right," Felton admitted. "You got it looking good, Oscar."

"You see all the posters we put up?" Oscar asked. "I got people trying to steal them. I sure wish you boys would sign some before tonight."

"Maybe we'll give some away," suggested Sonny. "And we've got a couple hundred eight-by-tens of Felton on his motorcycle."

"Great God," exclaimed Oscar. "They'll be fighting over them, that's for sure. I can tell you one thing, it's all this town's been talking about for a month. Everybody's proud of Felton, and that's a fact. Up in Cuttercane, they're talking about putting up a road sign saying he was born there."

"That right?" Felton asked with surprise.

"What I hear," Oscar replied. "They're all like me. I can't wait to see the picture. It's got a good story."

"I've got the film right here," Sonny said, tapping the canisters. "We'll thread it up about an hour before showtime. Until then, it stays with me." He paused, leaned close to Oscar. "There was some talk around Athens that it might be stolen. I can't let that happen."

"That right?" said Oscar. "Great God, it must be something."

"It is, Oscar, it is," Felton said proudly, cuffing Oscar on his shoulder. "What it's got is your name. It's got Oscar all over it."

Clara Weaver had cooked a twelve-course meal for Sonny and Felton. She called it a pre-premiere dinner. She had everything from quail to barbecue.

"Mama, there's just the two of us," Felton said gently.

"But you're stars," Clara cooed. "Stars can't go without having a selection of things to eat."

"Mama, we not that hungry," Felton protested.

"Then just take a bite of whatever you want," urged Clara. "Rabe can eat the leftovers."

"Where is Rabe?" asked Felton.

Clara shook her head sadly. "Honey, he's just jealous. He went off to Atlanta this morning. Said he had some work to do, but he don't. He's just jealous. It breaks my heart to see him that way."

"That's all right, Mama," Felton said.

"Of course," Sonny added cheerfully. "We're just glad to be here. I've heard a lot about you, Mrs. Weaver."

"Honey, call me Clara. Everybody does."

Sonny laughed politely. He patted Clara on the arm. "All right, Clara. I'll do that."

"I hope Rabe don't show up drunk tonight," Felton said. "He does, Mama, and I'll have to do something about it."

"Honey, promise me you'll be a gentleman," Clara said. "I've got my Sunday School class coming to see you in the picture show."

Sonny choked on a bite of ham. He looked at Felton in horror.

"You all right, Sonny?" Felton asked.

Sonny nodded. He said to Clara, "Your Sunday School class?"

Clara smiled triumphantly. "Well, the truth be known, it's more like the whole church. They're as proud of Felton as I am. We had a prayer about him last week."

"Uh, that's—nice," Sonny said. He nudged Felton. "Look, we better get on back up to the theater," he added. "If we get caught in a crowd, we won't be able to thread the movie."

"You just got here," Clara said in a small, disappointed voice.

"Mama, Sonny thinks we better go on," Felton explained softly. "He knows what needs doing."

"Well, all right," Clara conceded. "Take something with you. I guess Rabe can eat the rest, or maybe I'll have the church people over later on."

"You need a ride, Mama?" asked Felton.

"I'm coming with the preacher, honey."

As they drove away from his mother's home in Cuttercane, Felton said, "What'd you want to leave so fast for, Sonny? We just got there."

"Felton, I'm not so sure your mother's church will understand this movie," Sonny said seriously.

84

"It's just a movie," Felton replied.

"Well, it's a little bit more than that," Sonny offered. "You see, when I went back and made some changes I, well, added a couple of things. Symbolism. It's got a lot of action, but it's also got a lot of symbolism and it may even be considered a little, well, racy."

"What's that mean?" Felton asked.

"Racy?" Sonny answered. "It's a little like risqué, but not the same thing. Still, it may seem that way, especially to a whole church."

"Sonny, what are you talking about?" Felton demanded. His voice was edgy.

"You remember that love scene between you and Connie, don't you?" Sonny said. "I'm talking about that kind of thing."

"I told everybody about that," Felton said. "Shoot, they can't wait to see it. Some of my buddies started sweating when I told them what happened, and one or two of them belong to Mama's church."

"Maybe I'm wrong," Sonny muttered. "I hope so."

The Silver Screen Movie Palace was mobbed by six-thirty and the film was not scheduled to begin until eight. Oscar had rented two klieg lights from Gainesville and the lights panned the sky with criss-crossing beams. The Hiawassee High School band played John Philip Sousa march tunes from the sidewalk in front of the theater. Hired teenagers held signs that read: *Welcome Lone Biker!* The crowd, waiting anxiously, was dressed in Sunday clothing. They celebrated in loud, laughing voices.

Sonny had arranged with Oscar to have Felton arrive on a borrowed Harley-Davidson as the Lone Rider, complete with mask. Officers of the Hiawassee Police Department would lead him through the city with sirens blaring, then they would part the crowds for him and Felton would make a triumphant entry into the theater.

"It'll be a night to remember," Oscar predicted.

"I think you're right," Sonny said quietly.

"You ready to thread up?" asked Oscar.

"Might as well," Sonny replied.

At seven-thirty, Felton arrived to loud cheering. He had added a yellow neck scarf to his costume and the scarf waved like a flag in the night air. He vaulted from his borrowed motorcycle and threw the scarf around his neck in another loop. Then, waving to the cheering crowd, he entered the theater in a stride that would have made Ursula Bernhard weep with pride. Clara Weaver cried aloud, "That's my son. That's my son."

Inside, Sonny met Felton by the popcorn stand.

"Now, Felton, I don't think I told you this," Sonny said, "but it's bad luck for the star and the director to watch a movie with the crowd. We'd better go up in the projection booth."

"Won't nobody see us if we're up there," Felton protested.

"Well, now, I guess they won't, but we can't take the chance on bad luck, can we?" Sonny said.

"I guess not," Felton grumbled.

The movie began promptly at eight o'clock to a standing-room-only audience.

The first scene showed a strange light, like a swinging light bulb on a drop cord, floating across the screen. There was a weird, scratching sound of music and eerie, hooting cries, and then an explosion and the screen billowed full of smoke.

"What's that?" Felton asked in the projection booth.

"Uh, one of the changes I made," explained Sonny. "It's symbolism, Felton." Sonny was sweating profusely. His white suit was stained under his armpits.

Suddenly the figure of something resembling a satyr rose out of the smoke. He had the grotesque face of Satan. His body was covered with a red slime that stuck to him like paint. Worms that looked like maggots crawled in the slime. In the background there was the sound of a barking dog. The creature turned toward the sound.

"What's that?" demanded Felton.

"Evil, Felton," Sonny said. "That is the man called Evil. Evil in the flesh."

The screen did a jump-cut to a small, shaggy brown dog racing over the ground and then leaping through the air.

The screen did another jump-cut to the man called Evil as he reached out and caught the dog in mid-air and lifted it and then bit into the dog's neck. Blood gushed over the face of Evil.

Margaret Odom, who taught English at Hiawassee High School, threw up on her husband, Harry.

The crowd oohed restlessly.

"My God," Felton whispered. He turned to Sonny. "What's going on here?" he demanded.

"Uh, it's one of the changes I made," Sonny told him.

"Sonny, I'm gonna whip your ass," Felton hissed.

"Now, hold on, Felton. This is called scene setting. We needed it."

"How'd you do all that without me?" Felton wanted to know.

"Editing, Felton. You can do anything with a few feet of new film. You'll see."

"It better get around to me in a minute," Felton growled.

The film did get to Felton, or to Bret Holley, a.k.a. the Lone Biker, but it was not from the screenplay Felton had read.

Sonny had added another plot. The Lone Biker was not a human being at all, but a cosmic child who represented the heroic soul of goodness, and his battling of the motorcycle gang was merely child's play compared to his eternal fight with the slime-covered man named Evil.

The Lone Biker was a farce. It had scenes that made people gag and race from the theater to throw up on the sidewalk outside. It had moments—serious moments—that were funnier than Groucho Marx. The jousting-with-switchblades scene had been moved upfront in the story and had been cleverly edited to have the Lone Biker battling Evil, and the love scene between Connie and Felton had been altered to show Connie's tongue sliding down Felton's throat—or the throat of some actor who had been hired for a substitute scene—and Connie, or Karen, was seen swooning at the feet of the slime-covered man named Evil, giving in to him, making silhouetted love to him in the shadow of an oak.

"Sonny," Felton whispered, "I'm gonna whip your ass. I can hear my mama crying down there."

"You've got to see the symbolism in it," begged Sonny. "That man is sin, Felton, and he'll always be sin, and Karen's somebody lusting after sin, like people have been doing since Adam and Eve. That's why she can't have the Lone Biker. He's good through and through. That's you, Felton."

"This movie," Felton snarled, "ain't worth a pinch of owl shit. Ask Oscar. He'll tell you."

Oscar did not answer. Oscar had fainted on the projection room floor.

In the audience, Clara Weaver wept into the preacher's shoulder. The preacher prayed aloud. The Hiawassee High School band laughed idiotically. Some of the men who had been childhood friends with Felton, began to hoot his name: "*Felton, Felton, Felton...*"

Someone yelled, "Felton, you ought to be ashamed of yourself, boy." Felton recognized the voice. It was Rabe. Rabe was drunk.

The exclusive world premiere of *The Lone Biker* was over. The mayor demanded that the police confiscate the film and remove Sonny Paul Davis and Felton Eugene Weaver from the theater.

Felton slipped out of the back of the theater as the crowd gathered at the box office, demanding a refund of their money. He stole the borrowed motorcycle he had used for his grand entry and rode it back to California, where he resumed his old job as a driver for the Star Wheels Limousine Service. He changed his public name to Leonard Slye.

In time, Felton and Sonny resumed their friendship and they talked often about their experience with *The Lone Biker*.

"We was something," Felton suggested. "We was something else."

"We were ahead of our time," Sonny said philosophically. "That's what we were. We were trendsetters, but nobody knew it. Look at all those horror movies people are making today. Who got it started? We did, Felton. We did."

"Yeah, I guess so," Felton admitted, "but I never did see it from start to finish, from git-go to The End."

"I guess nobody in America did, other than me," said Sonny. "But it's not that bad. I mean, at least we did it. We could have wasted our lives beating around the bushes and talking about things, but we didn't; we tried. We made a movie. How many people can say that, Felton? How many people from God-forsaken Cuttercane, hillbilly Georgia, ever star in a movie? You, Felton. You. You're it."

Felton nodded a satisfied nod. "You got me there, Sonny, but I still can't go home. My mama says they still got my pictures up on some fence posts."

"Aw, they'll get over it," said Sonny. "They always do. In a couple of years, they'll be laughing about it."

"They already are," Felton mumbled.

"Give it time, Felton. Give it time," advised Sonny. "They'll see I'm right. We were just ahead of our time, that's all."

"What'd you do with that thing, anyhow?" asked Felton.

Sonny laughed. He raised a glass of beer in salute. "Sold it to a bunch of amateurs in Japan," he said. "They think they got a classic."

"You're a sly old dog, Sonny," Felton drawled. "Yes, you are. And you know what's funny about all that?"

"What?" asked Sonny.

"You and me both pulled a fast one on the Japanese. Remember me telling you about that Jap soldier I traded the Jeep to?"

Sonny hooted. "I'll be damned, Felton. You're right. Maybe that's what we ought to do. Maybe we ought to set ourselves up to deal with the Japanese for American companies." He laughed again. "We got the experience for it."

In Japan, *The Lone Biker* became a hit, a cult film highly praised for its remarkable symbolism. It had a spin-off of books and a staged musical. There were Lone Biker conventions. Thousands of Lone Biker imitation motorcycles roared over Japanese roads.

And there was one reviewer with a revealing line: "Felton Weaver," he wrote, "reminded me of the great American cowboy, Randolph Scott."

Founders (Without the Apostrophe) Day, 1955

The Story of
Elmo Parker and Monroe Dawson

In the beginning, there had been a debate about the wording of Founders Day in Claybank: Did Founders need an apostrophe, and, if so, where should it be placed—before or after the s?

It required two years of discussion to put the quarrel to rest. In the first year of celebration—in 1933—the apostrophe had been placed before the s, making it Founder's Day. In 1934, the apostrophe was placed after the s, proclaiming it as Founders' Day. The change from before to after had resulted in an impolite disagreement (a hair-pulling, said some) between Mildred Detwilder and Thelma Pearson, the two normally civilized teachers of English in the Claybank school system. Mildred had insisted her rules of grammar placed the apostrophe before the s, while Thelma's findings had it located in the after position. Mildred had claimed Thelma was too dumb to diagram a simple sentence and therefore knew nothing about the possessive case. Thelma supposedly retaliated by producing one of Mildred's college essays marked with the grade of a D, an essay with enough redlined corrections to give it the look of terminal measles.

In 1935—with the Mildred-Thelma embarrassment still lingering—the City Council had taken a recorded vote on the matter, electing to eliminate the apostrophe altogether. The consensus had been stated by then Council president Wayne Breedlove. "You can't hear it when you say it," Wayne had reasoned, "so they's no reason in writing it down."

Founders Day was sponsored by the Claybank City Council on the second Saturday of each April, and though it was not advertised as such, Founders Day had about it the nature of a pagan ritual of peculiar behavior performed by skimpily dressed ancient Greeks. It was spring and the Earth Animal was awake and restless, rising up from the hibernation of winter with a quivering of need. It was the season of the mystic, of something that had a scent of perfume about it, yet more intoxicating. It was the new skin of all senses—tender, quick, a begging to be realized in experiences never before tried.

Founders—without the apostrophe—Day was a ritual of becoming and of being.

However, none of the citizens of Claybank gave much thought to the Greeks or the Earth's swelling with new life, or imaginary scents. The citizens of Claybank celebrated Founders Day because it recognized the birthday of General Assay Claybank, hero of the American Revolution, founder of the township of Claybank and father of Claybank County. And it did not matter that Assay Claybank's credentials had been severely reviewed in 1931 in a study released by the Department of History at the University of Georgia.

The study charged that Assay Claybank was not a general of the American Revolution, was not a hero of any sort, and, indeed, had not founded Claybank.

Assay Claybank, the study revealed, had been a coward, a thief and, most notably, a liar. He had lied his way into the ownership of a small log store by claiming kinship to the owner, a feeble and forgetful man named Robert Brooks, and then he had lied his way into prominence by declaring exaggerated bravery in far-off battles, insisting that people address him as General Claybank. The University study scoffed at his claims, accusing him of being a runaway from a minor skirmish in Pennsylvania, but the University was late in its findings: Assay Claybank had bragged that he was a general, and people had believed him. From a portrait hanging in the county courthouse, he had had the look of a general—a frowning face with narrow eyes and thin lips, the portrait bearing a curious similarity to George Washington. And he had had a sword that a general would own. And he rode a horse that seemed several breeds above that of a common soldier. Thus, when a name was needed to mark the settlement that began to circle the log store he had acquired by deceit, Assay Claybank's name had been selected. Later, an act of the state legislature appointed his name as the county designation, solely on the recommendation of a committee chaired by Assay Claybank.

To the people of Claybank county, the myth surrounding Assay Claybank was firm and unshakeable. No one believed the University of Georgia's Department of History. The professors there were arrogant and narrow-minded. Everyone knew that. Besides, the professors did not teach history; they taught slander. It was rumor that some of them had actually informed students that Thomas Jefferson was the father of mulattos, a bastardly accusation made by the only true bastards associated with the story.

In an interview for the *Claybank Journal*, Wayne Breedlove had answered the University of Georgia's charges against Assay Claybank in a blistering retort: "They ought to mind their own damn business and quit fooling around in the past lives of people. We know who Assay Claybank was. Claybank's a good name over here."

It was two years later that Founder's Day was inaugurated, followed by Founders' Day, then by Founders Day.

Founders Day was divided, by tradition, into Day Things and Night Things, and that was the way the agenda of events was published by Happy Colquitt in the *Claybank Journal's* special Founders Day issue. It was always the largest issue of the *Journal* because Happy tormented every business establishment in Claybank until he had assurances of what he termed patriotic advertising.

Day Things included a sidewalk rummage-and-cake sale by the Women's Union of Christian Service, a non-denominational Protestant body organized and guided by Hilda Phillips, a stern woman with a man's hard features. There was always a declamation competition in the high school auditorium on the subject, "What Claybank Means to Me." There had never been more than twenty people who endured the competition from start to finish, including kin of the participants.

Other Day Things included early morning field events for grades five through eight, sponsored by the Claybank Elementary School. In the afternoon, there was a baseball game between the Claybank Textile Tigers and the Claybank High School Gladiators. The Tigers never lost. In fact, the Tigers had never been scored upon by the Gladiators. People in the know—those who read books—had long called the game comic relief because it was so laughable.

The most popular event of Day Things was the public display of the fire truck, waxed to a mirror shine. The fire truck was available for riding children around Courthouse Square and as a background for family photographs. Always, there was a false fire alarm at some predetermined location in mid-afternoon and the crowds cheered as the fire truck roared away, siren blaring.

Day Things were celebrated in a high-pitch mood of exuberance, as though all conventions of private restrictions had been pardoned and gloom, in whatever measure, had been temporarily put aside for the zeal that could be plucked from the day like grapes from a vine. There was no end to the noise, the blending of ladyish laughter and childish squealing and the bass counterpoint of men roaring over punch lines of mumbled jokes about forbidden fantasies of erotic pleasure. There was color and clearness to the day. It was an unbelievable fact, but it had never rained in Claybank County on Founders Day. It was as though someone had signed a long-term contractual agreement with God, one that permitted rain on the day before or the day after, but never on Founders Day. That fact was as dependable as the assurance that the Tigers would mercilessly slaughter the Gladiators.

Night Things for Founders Day was highlighted by a barbecue on the high school football field and a banquet in the high school auditorium.

The well-to-do, or those posing as the well-to-do, went to the banquet, though none of them wanted to be there, not with the scent of barbecue floating in the evening air.

Regular people—the great majority—went to the barbecue, many of them arriving from long drives out of surrounding counties. The out-of-county crowd had no interest in Claybank County's Founders Day; it was the barbecue that attracted them. They knew Emmett Mulherne would be supervising the cooking, and nobody on God's Earth, or in the history of God's time, knew as much about pork as Emmett. There were people who claimed that Emmett could cook a pig's oink worth serving as a delicacy to the Queen of England.

"That boy," the people declared, "has got the gift. Yes, he has."

What Emmett actually had was a secret sauce, a concoction that had people salivating from a two-mile radius of his cooking pot. The sauce was reddish-brown and thick. It had a sweet mustard odor and when it was swabbed over a plate of pulled loin or smoked ribs, it caused people to moan in awe. Mixed with Brunswick stew, it was the elixir of gladness.

The only drawback to attending one of Emmett's barbecues was in having to listen to him.

He had a high-pitched, whining voice and he told mean stories.

One such story was of his wife, Anna Cora Mulherne, a toothless woman who sat in a rocker and never spoke to anyone.

"That there woman," Emmett would say, pointing a stick of split hickory at Anna Cora, "ain't never loved nothing about me, excepting my barbecue. She's a fool about my cooking, ain't you, old woman?"

Anna Cora would not reply, would not move.

"Tell you how she come to meet up with me," Emmett would continue. "I was cooking up near Rabun Gap one day—about the time Adam first started putting up with Eve—and her and this old boy—he was a Whitworth—come by in a buggy and she smelt my sauce just riding along in the air and she made that Whitworth boy stop and get her a plate. And that, by God, done it. Next day, she come back by herself. Had her stuff in a fertilizer sack. Been around ever since. Couldn't run her off with a shotgun. Didn't make much difference back then. Lord, she used to be pretty as a magazine picture, but she ain't much to look at now, toothless old woman. Done gnawed them teeth right off, eating them smoked ribs. Yeah, I seen that old Whitworth boy two, three years ago, up at a cooking near to Gainesville. He bought me a bottle of store liquor just for taking that old woman off his hands. I drunk it up, too, didn't I, old woman? Me'n that Whitworth boy got ourselves drunker'n skunks. Ain't that right? Old woman's deaf as a fence post."

Anna Cora never changed expressions as Emmett talked. She had heard the story hundreds of times. If she had been pretty— magazine-picture pretty—it was in a lost past.

The Night Things banquet was for the purpose of honoring the Claybank Citizen of the Year. Its menu was a tribute to nourishment—fruit cups (each topped with a perfect maraschino cherry), salad in a side dish, English peas, creamed potatoes with an optional gravy pool, carrots (for color), and a main-course beef, usually a choice ribeye steak. The meal was prepared by the home economics class, with watchful participation by the three regular cooks for Claybank High School.

Inevitably, those who attended the banquet stopped later at Emmett's barbecue.

To socialize, they lied pleasantly.

To review the turnout.

To see if Emmett needed anything.

Emmett knew what they wanted: barbecue. And for that purpose, he always reserved one or two select shoulders cooking slowly over low-heat coals.

Historically, the Citizen of the Year banquet had been the most ignored event of Founders Day. It was only an occasion, an obligatory event for people with obligatory standing in the community. Only one recipient of the Citizen of the Year award had ever been remembered. In 1938, Otwell Yates, a banker, had been arrested by Federal authorities on a charge of forgery three days after being honored as Claybank's leading citizen for his sponsorship of an Honesty-in-Business civic campaign. Each year following, the chairman of the Citizen of the Year nominating committee issued the same warning: "Let's be particular. Remember Otwell Yates."

Founders Day for the city of Claybank in Claybank County of northeast Georgia was very much the same as every celebration for every town in the nation—a show-off day having the feel of a homemade circus, a routine of monotony that was pleasant enough, but still lacking in the fever pitch of roiled-up excitement.

In 1955, that changed for Claybank.

At the urging of Happy Colquitt, the City Council voted to end the annual mismatch of men versus boys in the baseball game between the Claybank Textile Tigers and the Claybank High School Gladiators. Instead the Tigers would play a worthy opponent, a team with drawing power. Happy railed that it would double attendance for the game and, therefore, would double spending potential for Founders Day business. For members of the City Council, it was a persuasive argument; they were all merchants.

"Somebody's got to be responsible," said Councilman Seth Pennefeather.

"Happy brought up the idea, let him do it," suggested Councilman Whitman Robart.

And Happy Colquitt, publisher, editor, writer, advertising manager, typesetter, and printer of the *Claybank Journal*, was appointed honorary commissioner for the First Annual Founders Day Semi-Professional Baseball Game.

It was a duty that Happy accepted seriously. He said to the Council, "You are about to have the damnedest baseball game you have ever seen on God's good earth."

"Now, Happy, don't get too carried away," advised Seth in his gentle manner. "Things have a way of backfiring. Keep Otwell Yates in mind."

"That's right," added Whitman. "Just a nice afternoon with lots of people showing up. That's all we want." He laughed. "Sounds to me like you thinking about bringing in the New York Yankees."

"Better than that," Happy replied confidently. "You'll see. I'm going to put together a game that'll bring people from a hundred miles away. I guarantee it."

Happy was not bragging. Though he had never played baseball, he knew it was a game of imagination and controversy as well as skill. And Happy was an expert in the use of imagination and controversy; he had been a journalist for thirty years.

Happy also knew there were only two teams in northeast Georgia that would encourage people to lie, cheat, or steal to find the price of admission for a game played between them.

And that was what Happy wanted.

It would be the most talked-about event in Claybank since the ceremonial burying of the textile union in 1951, and it would provide Happy with enough material for several banner headlines.

One team was certain. The host team. The Claybank Textile Tigers, managed by Elmo Parker.

Elmo had been born north of Claybank in the small community of Cuttercane. By the age of fifteen he had attracted baseball scouts from as far away as New York and Detroit. Not a boy alive, and few men, could throw a baseball as fast, or as accurate, as Elmo Parker at age fifteen. He was, said the scouts who saw him, a future star. *Bona fide*. Elmo had signed with the Brooklyn Dodgers at the age of sixteen, but two years later had returned to Cuttercane homesick and confused by the strange behavior of fans at Ebbets Field. "They crazy," had been his assessment.

At the age of twenty-five, after years of textile mill games, he had signed with the Chattanooga Lookouts. In 1946, he set a league record by striking out eighteen men in a row—five on the minimum of three pitches. Tragically, a flung bat had crushed a bone in the elbow of his pitching arm in 1947 and his career as a pitcher was over. He had converted to first base, but did not have the fielding grace or the power at bat to play regularly and at the beginning of 1950, he had retired from baseball as a player. That spring, he had been hired by Ralph Claybank, descendent of Assay Claybank and second-generation owner of Claybank Textiles, Inc., to manage the company's baseball team, called the Tigers, and also to work in the shipping department during the off-season. The team he had inherited had been laughable, except for the annual game against the high school Gladiators, and he had wasted no time in changing the team's attitude and record. A large, brooding, resentful man, Elmo did not accept relaxed losing as an alternative to determined winning, and in two years' time, the Tigers won the Savannah River Mill League championship, mainly in defense against Elmo's temper.

The success of the Tigers, reasoned Happy, would be the perfect bait for his perfect game. And in Happy's way of thinking, the Tigers could not refuse to play. It was their patriotic duty.

Still, Happy knew Elmo.

Elmo would explode.

Happy laughed at the thought as he called Ralph Claybank.

Ralph Claybank's office was the most expensive room in Claybank. Its design and decoration had been copied from a photograph in *Esquire* magazine by an interior designer in Atlanta who had gained a minor reputation among the Atlanta elite for his bold use of color and lighting. Male employees of Claybank Textiles, Inc., who had seen photographs of the office, called it the Ladies Room. They also called Ralph Claybank a lady, a snickering put-down that carried uncomfortable insinuations. Reasonable-thinking people—those in high-management positions—did not condemn Ralph merely because he was not married and tended to be a little prissy, or because he spent almost every weekend in either Atlanta or Athens. To reasonable-thinking people in high-management positions, Ralph was simply refined. After all, he had been to Rome, Italy, and Paris, France, and Brussels, Belgium, and he could say "Good morning" in five languages other than English.

The office had the dark look of coffee with contrasting gold streaks accented by pools of recessed lighting. The furniture seemed oversized, as though expecting a man larger than Ralph to occupy it. Sitting behind his desk in a leather chair taller than his head, positioned under a lightfall from a recessed bulb, Ralph looked sinister.

Elmo Parker sat uncomfortably in a chair at one corner of the desk, facing Ralph. Elmo did not belong in the room. He was out of place, and he knew it. Happy sat at the opposite corner of the desk, leaning forward in his chair, staring across the space of light pools and shadows. He could not see Ralph's eyes because of the light and the tall leather chair that pulled Ralph into its deep tan color.

"The way I see it," explained Happy, "we got a chance to make Founders Day something special again, something that'll draw people from as far away as Anderson, South Carolina, and maybe even from Atlanta. That's why the Council made up its mind to change the baseball game."

"We're happy to help out where and when we can," Ralph said cheerfully from his leather-chair hiding. His voice was as small as his body. "Claybank Textiles always supports local enterprise," he added.

"Well, Ralph, I know that," Happy replied. "You put the biggest ad in the paper every year for Founders Day. Always giving to help out at the rummage sale and I know it's you that pays to have the fire truck waxed. But what I'm talking about is different."

"Sounds enticing," said Ralph. He twisted in his chair and tapped his fingertips together like an excited child.

"The fact is, baseball's bigger than it ever was," continued Happy. "Got more people going to games, more people talking about it. Am I right about that, Elmo?"

"I guess," mumbled Elmo. Elmo had never trusted Happy. Happy's accounts of the Tigers' baseball games in the *Claybank Journal* had always been absurd.

"Right as right can be," emphasized Happy. "Yessir. And if you do it up special, that'll bring more people out than you can shake a stick at. That's why they got them all-star games and the World Series. Do it up special and you'll get the people."

"Well, Mr. Colquitt, that makes perfect sense," agreed Ralph. "Personally, I'm not a great fan of the sport, but I have friends who are and my father enjoyed watching games. I keep the team in his memory. Besides, I'm told it's good for morale." He paused and Happy imagined that he smiled. Then he said, "Now, exactly what is it that you want our lads to do?"

He's got to be a woman wearing a man's suit, thought Happy. No one called baseball players lads. A baseball player would slap a man silly for calling him a lad.

"Play this special game on Founders Day," Happy answered.

"I see, I see," Ralph said seriously. He again tapped his fingertips together and leaned back in his chair. The lightfall above him struck his frail chest, and a sparkle from a jeweled tie tack blinked in the dark room.

"Just like you've always been doing, every year," Happy said quickly, "only this time you won't be playing the high school team."

"You want our lads to play someone else?" asked Ralph.

Happy smiled. He squinted his eyes to find Ralph's face. He could not. "That's right," he said easily.

"Who we supposed to be playing?" Elmo asked suspiciously.

Happy smiled again. "The Jefferson Bluejays," he said.

Elmo pulled himself to the edge of his chair. His face sagged, his eyes widened. "Niggers?" he said incredulously.

"Colored," Happy answered in an easy manner.

"You gone slap crazy, Happy?" Elmo stammered.

"It's the only team around that can give you a game, and you know it," Happy snapped. "You not afraid of playing a colored team, are you? They got colored boys in the big leagues now."

"Afra—?" Elmo could not finish the word. The blood of temper pumped across his face.

"Now, now, Elmo," Ralph said in a soothing voice. "Don't get bothered by what Mr. Colquitt said without considering its merits. Flying off at the handle is much worse than dilly-dallying. As a matter of fact, Mr. Colquitt might have a splendid idea."

"Mr. Claybank, my boys don't play no colored teams," Elmo said firmly.

"Now, that simply isn't true, Elmo," Ralph replied, swiveling in his chair to face Elmo. "You play two or three practice games every spring against the Negro Mill League in South Carolina, I understand."

"But them's practice games; that ain't in-season," Elmo protested.

Ralph laughed a silly, high, rolling laugh. "Elmo," he said, "that's the most ridiculous thing I've heard anyone utter in a month of Sundays. You mean there's a difference?"

"But—but it ain't done," Elmo cried.

"Doesn't mean it can't be done, now does it?" countered Ralph, shaking a skinny finger from the pit of his chair. "Why if my ancestor, General Claybank, had been so narrow-minded he might never have routed the British in our great Revolutionary War and we'd all be answering to kings and queens and all those other royals." He stood and began pacing the room, pausing under the spotlights. His head was bowed in thought. "Frankly," he finally said, "it may be an excellent idea, Mr. Colquitt. It could show we're not the primitives people think we are, and with the Supreme Court's decision last year, we're going to be put under the microscope, so to speak. My friends in Atlanta keep warning me about that." He moved to another spotlight, stopped and paused like a male model on a turn. "And, indeed, it could be one of the biggest things we've ever done to draw attention to Founders Day. My father would have liked that. I remember him talking about the Jefferson Bluejays. He made them sound fierce."

Fierce? Godalmighty, Happy thought. *Fierce?*

"It sounds like an absolutely grand idea," Ralph added eagerly, moving in a dance step to the side of his desk.

"Well, I appreciate your support," Happy told him. "And your daddy knew what he was talking about when he said the Bluejays were good. Even Elmo knows that."

Ralph pushed up on tiptoe and pulled himself to a sitting position on the edge of the desk. His feet dangled above the floor. He peered at Elmo. "Well?" he said. "Is that true? About the caliber of the Bluejays' team?"

Elmo was confused and angry. "They may be good, but, dammit, they's colored and this ain't the time to play no colored teams. They'd be trouble, and I guarantee it."

"Could you beat them in a contest?" asked Ralph.

Elmo's eyes narrowed. His face was hard and determined. He looked once at Happy, then back to Ralph. "Damn right we could," he growled. "Beat their ass seven ways to Sunday."

Ralph smiled the smile of an excited child. "I expect you to," he said pleasantly.

"They ain't seen the day they can whip my boys," Elmo snarled, fighting to control his anger. He glared at Happy. "And I don't give a damn what nobody says."

Happy offered a smile in return. He knew that Elmo was temporarily blinded by pride and temper, and possibly fear. The lowdown on the Jefferson Bluejays of 1955 went far beyond bragging: the Jefferson Bluejays of 1955 could beat the combined squads of the Brooklyn Dodgers and the New York Yankees nine out of ten times.

"I like that spirit, Elmo," Happy said. "I surely do."

The Jefferson Bluejays did not belong to a mill league, or to any league of any description.

The Bluejays played any team foolish enough to take the field against them.

Baseball was the Bluejays' sense of identity, a relief from anonymity, and the players played the game with the passion and strategy and stubbornness of war. The team had been founded in 1926 by a rare man named Monroe Dawson, who was then twenty-six years old. The Bluejays had never had another manager and at age fifty-five, Monroe ran his team with such absolute authority that anyone who argued unwisely with him would be swiftly and harshly judged by a small army of supporters expert in administering effective punishment. Monroe regarded such action as his check-and-balance system.

Many of Monroe's players had been trained from childhood to believe the ultimate honor in life was a hand-down uniform emblazoned with the word *Bluejays* across the chest. A starting berth on the team earned privileges in the black community of Jefferson that no other distinction equaled, and to assure a proper attitude of competition, Monroe had never assigned a position until there had been a blood duel over the matter. All positions were open—except for catcher. Monroe was the catcher for the Bluejays. Even at age fifty-five, no one dared challenge Monroe, though he did have to negotiate certain stipulations not customary in baseball. First, as catcher, Monroe could sit on a small, three-legged milking stool, and, second, if he got a hit during a game, he could have a pinch-runner without being removed from play.

"It's my legs," Monroe would explain in a slow, pitiful voice. "They's gone. Old man can't get around no more."

In exchange for these exceptions to the accepted order of the game, Monroe agreed not to pitch Washington Doubletree during the first three innings of a game.

It was a generous offer.

Washington Doubletree could throw a baseball through a sheet of steel.

A popular tall tale had it that no one had ever seen a ball leave Washington Doubletree's hand during a pitch. Not even Monroe. Monroe simply positioned his catcher's mitt where he desired the pitch and Washington threw it as instructed. There was a rumor that umpires did not watch for Washington's pitch; they watched Monroe's mitt. If the mitt carried left, right, up or down on impact, the pitch was believed to be a ball. If Monroe sank straight back on his stool, it was a strike.

Among the blacks who watched Washington pitch, there was no doubt that Satchel Paige had played softball in a girls' league by comparison. Washington had a presence on the mound that inspired awe. He would stand as erect as an English butler announcing company. Then, before each pitch, he would present the ball to the hitter as though holding an egg for inspection. A sneer would crack across his scarred face—the scar being from a jailhouse fight during his early twenties. He would bend forward at the waist in a stiff, polite bow. His right arm would rise slowly as he rocked backward and the ball would disappear into the curl of his hand like a swallowed marshmallow. He would spin, pause, hurl himself forward and his arm would whip through the air like an infuriated snake and his hand would slap hard against his chest. In almost the same instant, Monroe would moan with the force of the ball burying into his mitt.

Washington Doubletree was more than a pitcher; Washington Doubletree was an intimidator.

Happy Colquitt knew all of this about the Jefferson Bluejays. He knew of Monroe Dawson and of Washington Doubletree and of all the other players whose lives were fashioned by the hand-down uniforms with the stitching of *Bluejays* on the chest.

And it took him no more than ten minutes with Monroe to settle the matter of the Claybank Textile Tigers playing the Jefferson Bluejays on April 9, 1955, at the Claybank High School baseball field—a game that would include the special conditions proposed by Monroe.

"I'm telling you," Happy bragged to anyone who would listen. "You ask anybody that knows diddley from squat, we'll be turning them away a day ahead of time. Truth be known, I'd rather have this game than the World Series."

And to those who bellowed about whites playing against blacks, Happy tap-danced around the issue by claiming the real reason he had concocted the game was to teach colored people a thing or two about their place in life.

"They need to be taken down a couple of notches," said Happy.

"Well, that's a fact," said the grumblers.

"Still, it'll be a helluva game," Happy predicted. "Yes sir, a helluva game." No one knew why he laughed when he said such things.

April 9, 1955. Saturday. Nine-fifteen, a.m.

Emmett Mulherne scrubbed the ache from his face at the spigot beside the concession stand on the Claybank High School football field. He needed rest. He had been awake through the night, moving large boulders of pork across a wide steel grate, punching, spearing, testing, keeping the meat turned and hissing with grease drops melting from the bone-center of the cuts. He had performed the ritual of his barbecue for so many years he had learned to cook from the sound of fat drippings spewing on hickory coals. It was, to Emmett, a kind of Morse Code, the dots and dashes of emergency signals that only he could intercept and only he could decipher. At nine-fifteen, a.m., Saturday, April 9, 1955, Emmett knew he could rest. He knew by the sound and by the taste of a pinched-away bite of pork shoulder.

"Getting right, boys," Emmett said to DeWitt Mahan and Henry Weeks, his chief assistants for fifteen years. DeWitt and Henry knew Emmett's habits and most of his cooking secrets, but they did not know the timing; they could not hear what Emmett heard in the sizzle of fat drippings or taste what Emmett tasted, even if they pretended to be his equal in the art of barbecuing pork over the embers of cured hickory scooped out of burn barrels and scattered under slabs of meat.

"Ooooh, wheeeee," said DeWitt, rapidly chewing a too-hot sampling. He smacked his lips, blew heat from his mouth, did a little dance step of approval, then added, "It's good, sure enough."

"You and Henry keep them last cuts pushed back over some low coals," Emmett said. "Them'll be for the late-comers." He looked again at the meat, at the glow of the coals. "Henry, you keep stirring the stew," he added. "Don't want it to scorch."

"That's the truth," said Henry in his soft drawl.

The water from the spigot had cleaned Emmett's face and cooled him, but it had not revived him. He needed sleep. Still, he knew he could not rest until everything was in order, and he did a slow walk around the work area he and DeWitt and Henry had established, inspecting the serving tables and the setup for paper plates and napkins and forks. His eyes scanned the location of garbage pails, which would invite the Feast of Leftovers from horseflies and gnats and yellow jackets. Emmett knew the pails would be toppled and rolled before the day was over, but they were now in order and that was his interest.

He moved slowly—as weary, older men move—to the foldout cot stationed beneath his lean-to of sheet tin. He sat on the edge of the cot and watched the Claybank Police Department's Ford entering the double gates of the fence surrounding the football field. Otha, he thought.

Otha Estes parked his police car beside the row of serving tables, and opened the car door and eased outside. He stood for a moment, stretching. A yawn broke across his mouth. He waved to DeWitt and Henry and strolled casually to Emmett. Otha was a tall, slender man with a face as hard as a stone carving.

"How's it going?" said Otha to Emmett.

"Good, going good," replied Emmett. "How you doing?"

"Doing good," said Otha. "Better than I ought to be, I guess." He looked skyward. "Got us a day for it," he added. "Thought it was about to wash us down the river for a while there last night."

"Uh-huh. It come down, all right, but it's daytime and it knows better than to rain in daytime," Emmett said.

Otha stretched again. He inhaled slowly, wagged his head in appreciation of the scent of cooked barbecue. "Smells good, Emmett, like it always does. I got a whiff a couple of blocks away."

"Better go get yourself a bite before it gets gone," advised Emmett. He bent forward slowly, unlacing his shoes and pushing them beneath the cot.

"Well, now, I think I will, Emmett. Not had breakfast yet," Otha said. He looked around the camp. "How's Anna Cora?" he asked. "I've not seen her around."

Emmett looked up. "She dead, Otha," he answered softly. "Passed on the first day of March."

Otha was shocked. He lowered his voice. "Didn't know that, Emmett. Sorry to hear about it."

Emmett nodded, the nods bringing a sag to his body. He said, "Old woman. Heart give out on her. She was in her rocker, rocking away. Weren't a sound out of her. Just quit rocking and bowed her head, like she was taking a nap."

"Won't be the same without Anna Cora around," said Otha.

"No, it ain't," Emmett whispered. Then: "You go over and tell DeWitt to cut you a hunk off a shoulder. I'm taking me a nap."

"You do that, Emmett," Otha said. "I'll be checking on things a little bit later. You need anything, let me know." He shook his head sadly. "Sure sorry to hear about Anna Cora."

Emmett rolled his body onto the cot and closed his eyes. He could hear Otha and DeWitt and Henry talking about barbecue and the afternoon game between the Tigers and the Bluejays. He thought of Anna Cora, dead in her rocker, propped from falling by the fat that rolled around her like a tire. He thought of the quick, slanting rain shower that had struck unexpectedly at three o'clock in the night—noisy, furious, yet playful, the rain splattering over the tin of his lean-to in a drumming that had always pleased him. Rain on tin was one of the best things he had ever known. He and Anna Cora had loved under that tin, rain raining like music, Anna Cora pretty as a magazine picture, balancing like a feather on the so-little room of the cot. A good memory it was. A good memory.

His eyes were heavy and burning. He blinked moisture into them.

And then he slept.

Happy Colquitt was in his office at the *Claybank Journal*, preparing for the day's events. His wife, Inez, was with him, watching as he cleaned the lenses of his cameras. No one irritated Happy as much as Inez. She said again and again, "What you want me to be doing, Happy, honey? You know I need supervision, so be sure and tell me."

"Inez," said Happy, "you just keep watch on the clock. It's that little thing over there on the desk. Goes tick-tick-tick. Got the big hand and the little hand."

"Happy, I know what a clock is."

"Well, watch it. I got things to do," Happy ordered. "We're going to be running around like a chicken with its head cut off. You wait and see. This game is going to go down in history." He picked up his Speed Graphic and examined it. "Yessir. It's going to be one for the ages."

"Honey, it's eighteen minutes after ten," Inez said sweetly.

"Jesus, Inez," Happy muttered wearily.

"You told me—"

"I know, I know."

"Is everything all right over at the ball park?" asked Inez.

"They better be," said Happy. "I saw some Boy Scouts over there earlier, setting up the concession stand. One of them had the flag—the James boy, one that's going to play the Anthem on his trumpet."

"He's sweet," cooed Inez.

"He's fat," countered Happy. "I saw him looking off toward Emmett's barbecue and drooling like a dog."

"Well, he can't help it," said Inez. "His mama and daddy are both oversized people. Bothers me just to look at them."

"Only thing that bothers me is Elmo," Happy offered. "Be just like him to take his team off somewhere else. Man like Elmo, you can't trust."

"Oh, Happy, that's a harsh thing to say. I'd think Mr. Claybank would have his job if he does something like that."

Happy snorted—a muffled, half-sneeze sound, a sound of habit over being excessively annoyed. Inez knew the warning.

"Honey, it's ten twenty-five," Inez said.

"Inez, shut up," Happy growled.

Otha Estes watched the traffic build in Claybank. He saw the growing mix of blacks and whites, hurriedly shopping or standing in segregated groups on street corners. He watched the fluttering hands of Hilda Phillips as she directed the rummage-and-cake sale sponsored by the Women's Union of Christian Service. He waved to Pete McKenzie as Pete lifted scurrying children onto and off the fire truck. Happy's boast of doubling traffic for Founders Day was conservative; Otha had never seen as many people in Claybank, not even to celebrate the end of World War Two. He knew that Happy's selection of the Bluejays to play the Tigers in the afternoon baseball game was the draw, not Hilda Phillips' Women's Union of Christian Service. And it wasn't the fact that one team was black and the other team white. Black teams and white teams occasionally played one another in pickup games, but such teams were mostly inferior and their following insignificant. The Bluejays and the Tigers, in a game shamelessly promoted by Happy, were another matter.

Otha saw Seth Pennefeather and Whitman Robart moving away from the cake sale, crossing the street, heading for their side-by-side furniture and clothing stores on Brinson Street. He eased the police car from Pittman's Service Station and drove along the street until he reached Seth and Whitman and slowed to a stop.

"How's it going?" Otha called through the rolled-down window on the front-seat passenger side.

Seth and Whitman paused.

"Going fine," Seth answered.

"Big crowd out," said Whitman.

"Biggest I ever saw," acknowledged Otha. "You boys going to be over at the game?"

"Wouldn't miss it," Seth told him.

"Happy would never speak to us again, if we did," Whitman added, laughing. "You been over there?"

"An hour or so ago," Otha replied. "Had some people already standing around, near the gate."

Seth stepped close to the car and leaned to the open window. He said in a serious manner, "You don't expect any trouble, do you?"

"Don't expect none," Otha said. "Why?"

"There's been some talk around," Seth told him. "Runt Ashford and that crowd."

"What kind of talk?"

"What you'd expect out of Runt," Whitman said. He looked to Seth. Seth nodded agreement.

"Well, you know Runt," said Otha.

"He was saying that Elmo had better take care of that colored team, or he would," Whitman offered.

Otha nodded. He could feel a wrinkle of worry folding into his brow. He knew that Compton Kent and Charles Doeman were somewhere in town. Compton and Charles made up the rest of the police force of Claybank. If there was trouble, he would need both

114

men, and maybe even the Georgia National Guard. Runt Ashwood was a mean little cockroach of a human being and he had a following of troublemakers that gave decency a bad name.

"I'll go find Compton and Charles," Otha said. "Have them around, just in case. But I wouldn't go worrying about Runt. He's just running off at the mouth, like he's always doing."

"Just don't want any trouble," said Seth. "Founders Day, you know."

Otha dipped his head, made a slight wave with his hand, and drove away. He found Compton and Charles at the Claybank Café, having coffee. He warned them about Runt.

"I'll bust his butt, he even looks like he's ready to start something," Compton said easily. "I hate that little bastard."

"Well, just keep a look out," Otha said. "I'm going over to the park. Game starts in a couple of hours."

At one-fifteen, there was a block-long waiting line at the Claybank High School baseball field admission gate. Inside, the bleachers were already filled, with a standing-room-only crowd taking its place along the first and third base foul lines—blacks on the third-base side and whites on the first-base side. A high, pushed-up dirt knoll left from scrapping out the field with bulldozers years earlier, was covered with people beyond the outfield fence—mostly black—sitting in cane-bottom chairs.

Otha's response was one of awe. He whispered to himself, "My God." Then he turned his attention to searching the crowd for Runt Ashford. The person he saw was Happy Colquitt, striding toward him wearing a proud, exuberant smile.

"What'd I tell you, Otha?" Happy exclaimed. "By God, I told you, didn't I?"

"Where'd they come from?" asked Otha. "They's more people here than they is in the whole county."

"You name it," Happy answered. "We got ten or twelve cars from over in South Carolina, one from Kentucky. I should've doubled the price." He turned to the crowd, made a sweeping wave with his arm. "Look at that," he added.

Otha scanned the gathering, still searching for Runt. The before-game festival of uninhibited gladness had the making of trouble, and he knew it. The sun was a ball of heat, cooking into the red clay dirt and scorched grass of the playing field. Far off, in the western corner of the adjacent football field, Emmett Mulherne's barbecue slow-cooked under slender ribbons of blue hickory smoke, the aroma sliding through the air like an intoxicating perfume.

"Yes sir," yodeled Happy. "Look up and down them foul lines, Otha. Black up third, white down first. That was my idea. Keep down trouble. But to tell you the truth, we may need the State Patrol for crowd control if folks keep coming."

"I think you got a point," admitted Otha.

The Claybank Textile Tigers were completing their infield warm-up when Otha moved through the crowd to find Elmo, who was standing beside the Tigers' bench, glaring at his team. Otha liked Elmo because Elmo did not tolerate nonsense. In Otha's way of thinking, Elmo would have made one hell of a policeman.

"You don't look too happy," Otha said.

"I ain't," Elmo said bluntly.

"Got a crowd, though," suggested Otha.

"Piss on it," Elmo snapped. "Ain't right playing colored teams after the season's got started."

"Yeah, well, maybe so, but it ain't nothing but a game," Otha reminded him.

"You seen Claybank?" Elmo asked suddenly, his voice low and angry.

"Not yet. He here?"

Elmo jerked his head toward the crowd. "Up yonder. Got some of his friends out from Atlanta. Brought them down here. Made me shake hands with them."

Otha turned inconspicuously and looked into the bleachers. He could see Ralph Claybank on the fourth row up, flanked by two men, one thin and pale, the other tall and muscular with a deep suntan. They were leaning close to Ralph, listening, laughing. The crowd around them was staring in disapproval.

"Oh, Lord," whispered Otha.

"I almost puked," said Elmo. He shook his head sadly.

"Well, they'll be gone when it's all over with," Otha counseled. He stepped close to Elmo. "Just wanted you to know there's some talk that Runt and his buddies might cause some trouble. But we'll take care of it."

"Sic them on Ralph," Elmo said bitterly.

"Come on, Elmo, forget that," Otha urged. "It's going to be a good game."

"Maybe."

"Good luck."

"Yeah."

Otha walked away toward the visitors' side of the field, to the bench were the Bluejays were patiently waiting and watching the infield work of the Tigers. Otha knew the crowd was watching him and he knew he had one chance to plea for sanity. He moved to Monroe Dawson, who was sitting on his three-legged catcher's stool. Monroe appeared older than Otha imagined he would be. His hair was close-cut and white and thinning. His face was puffed and lined. It was impossible to think of Monroe as a baseball player.

"Mr. Dawson," Otha said, "I'm Otha Estes, chief of police here in Claybank."

Monroe pulled himself slowly to a standing position. He extended his hand to Otha. "Glad to meet you," he said, smiling. His voice was deep and tired.

"Just want you to know how much we appreciate you coming over to play this game," Otha said. He could feel the steel in Monroe's grip.

"Ought to be a good one," Monroe remarked. He wagged his head like a man facing dread. "We been hearing a lot about your boys. Just hope y'all don't go whipping up on us too bad."

"I was about to ask the same thing," said Otha.

Monroe chuckled softly. The two men stood together, watching the last of Elmo's infielders sweep up a grounder and snap-throw it to the catcher at close range.

"Good crowd," said Otha.

Monroe scanned the stands. He nodded. "That's the truth," he said.

"You feel all right, being closed in like this?" asked Otha.

Monroe smiled. He knew what Otha was asking. "You ain't got to worry none," he said. "Me and my boys not expecting no trouble. No sir. We play lots of white boys. Don't have no trouble. It ain't nothing but baseball."

"We'll be on the watch," Otha said. "Good luck to you."

"Same to you," Monroe replied.

Otha walked along the Bluejays' bench, deliberately close. He nodded to each of the players and the players nodded in return. All were seated in absolute silence. All except Washington Doubletree. Washington Doubletree stood at the end of the bench, massaging a worn baseball in his massive right hand. Otha was awed by his size. Six feet, five inches. At least that. Maybe taller. Two hundred and fifty pounds, or maybe two-seventy. Muscle. All muscle. His body was as trim as a fighter's body—great, wide shoulders, slender waist, powerful thighs. A scar of pale purple ran across the dark ebony of his left cheek. His face was solemn, his eyes fixed on the pitcher's mound.

"How you doing?" Otha asked.

Washington Doubletree blinked. He nodded once.

Clyde Mayberry, who had been employed by Happy to umpire the game from behind home plate, introduced Elmo and Monroe to Reece Baldwin and Bobby Evans, who would call plays from the field.

"They's no special ground rules that I know of," said Clyde. "It's pure-T baseball. Only thing different—and I'm guessing you know about it, Elmo—is that Monroe gets to use him a stool when he's catching. And if he gets a hit, somebody else will be running for him."

"They told me," Elmo said coolly. "Just to make it clear, it won't be my fault if one of my boys slides into him on a play at home and he gets hurt."

Monroe smiled. "No sir, won't be nobody's fault but mine," he said. "I just appreciate it. Old as I am, I need some help."

"Washington can't do no pitching until the fourth inning," Elmo added. "That's the deal."

"That's right," agreed Monroe. "He gonna put hisself on the bench and he ain't gonna move."

"Let's play some baseball then," Elmo snapped. He whirled and walked away.

"Mr. Elmo," Monroe called. Elmo stopped and turned back.

"Good luck," Monroe said softly, smiling.

Otha positioned himself near the stands. He heard Happy talking excitedly to Ralph Claybank and he heard Ralph's shrill giggle in reply. And then he heard Inez: "Happy, honey, where am I supposed to be?" Otha thought: Thank you, Jesus, that somebody besides me is married to that woman. He turned to the field.

Sonny Jim Wallace worked his warm-up pitches for the Tigers. Sonny Jim was small. He wore glasses that were secured to his face by four rubber bands looped together and knotted on the ear-curve of the frames. His baseball cap was pulled to one side of his head, making him appear lopsided. Still, small as he was and with his lopsided look, Sonny Jim's motion from the mound was flawless, like a knife thrower at a county carnival. His pitches did not have speed; they had stuff. He did not strike out the opposition; he made the opposition hit the ball where he wanted it hit. It was a tale of local folklore that Sonny Jim had actually called the hits against a team from Gaffney, South Carolina.

Around Otha, the crowd began its overture of game noise.

"Attay, boy, Sonny Jim. Throw it in there."

"You the man, Sonny Jim. Can't hit what they can't see."

"Attay, babe. Attay, boy"

"Let's go, Tigers!"

Aubrey James, fifteen years old, Boy Scout, two hundred and thirty pounds, marched to the mound and faced home plate. He lifted his trumpet and began to play *The Star-Spangled Banner*, the flab on his body quivering in sync with the notes. The Tigers in the infield removed their caps and placed them over their hearts and stood as erect as soldiers. On the sidelines, the Jefferson Bluejays stood solemnly, staring at the flag being hoisted on the centerfield flagpole by two members of the Claybank High School baseball Gladiators, dressed in their game uniforms.

"That's nice," Seth Pennefeather whispered to Whitman Robart.

"It is," Whitman whispered in return.

A few voices, off key, began mumbling lyrics: *"...what so proudly we hailed at the twilight's last gleaming...."*

And then the game began.

Sonny Jim Wallace against Carver White, leadoff man and second baseman for the Bluejays.

Sonny Jim threw one pitch, a listless fastball intended as a teaser, and Carver hit a double down the first base line.

A few blacks applauded cautiously.

"Don't worry about it, Sonny Jim," the Tigers infielders shouted, springing on their toes, slapping dirt between their legs like playful monkeys. "Lucky hit, Sonny Jim. Lucky hit. You got 'em, babe. You got 'em, boy."

And Sonny Jim squinted his eyes to look into Moody Hickman's catcher's mitt. Moody flashed two fingers between his legs. Curve. Sonny Jim nodded gravely.

Alfred Oldfield was the batter. Alfred played first base for the Bluejays.

Sonny Jim turned to stare at Carver, leaning lazily off second. Carver had the loose moves of a dancer, his body poised on the balance of space between second and third base.

"Pissant," Sonny Jim mumbled. He began his motion, paused, kicked and threw to Alfred.

"Striiiike!" bellowed Clyde Mayberry.

Sonny Jim threw two more curves, dropping the ball two inches on each pitch. Alfred Oldfield struck out without moving the bat from his shoulder. He turned calmly on his spikes and strolled back toward the Bluejays' bench.

Monroe was standing in the on-deck circle, holding three bats in his hands. "What's he got?" he said quietly to Alfred.

"Nothing," whispered Alfred. "Little old dinky curve. Nothing."

"Uh-huh," Monroe said. He handed Alfred two of the bats.

The crowd was up, high on the beauty of Sonny Jim's strikeout. The crowd did not know that Alfred was a decoy for Monroe, the sacrifice who merely stood in judgment of Sonny Jim's ability.

"You got 'em, Sonny Jim!"

"Throw it in there, babe. Attay, boy!"

Monroe walked slowly to the batter's box. He nodded to Moody. "He looking good," Monroe said, motioning to Sonny Jim with his head. "Lordy, we ain't used to no curve-baller."

Moody knew he was being suckered. He watched Monroe bend painfully to pat his hands in the red dirt of the batter's box.

"Getting too old and that ain't no lie," Monroe added in a soft voice. "Can't move no more. Can't see nothing, and him throwing that curve ball. Lord, I might as well go find me a rocking chair, all the good I'be doing out here."

Moody's mind raced in strategy. If Monroe was complaining about a curve ball it was likely a set-up, a tease, a dare. Call for the curve ball and Monroe might be waiting on it and the damn thing might wind up in Kentucky. Fastball would be better.

Moody squatted behind home plate

No, he thought. Monroe had been around since Moses was a baby and he was sly as a fox. Monroe would guess fastball because a curve ball would be expected by the way he was teasing Moody. Doing the unexpected was the trick. Best to go with the curve ball, which would not be expected because Monroe would be thinking fastball after trying to fool Moody into thinking curve ball.

Moody shook his head, confused by his own reasoning. He looked up at Monroe. Monroe stood placidly at the plate, the bat leaning like a burden across his shoulder. Moody jabbed his hand between his legs. He flashed one finger. Fastball. Sonny Jim shook away the sign. Chickenshit, Moody thought angrily. He flashed for the fastball a second time, wagging his finger frantically. Again, Sonny Jim shook away the sign.

"Time," Moody called. He jogged to the mound. "What the hell you doing, Sonny Jim?" he demanded.

"Nothing," Sonny Jim said arrogantly. "I don't want that pitch."

Moody pushed his catcher's mask up, balancing it on his forehead. He said, "Sonny Jim, that ain't my pecker that's dangling down. That's the damn fastball sign and when I say throw it, you damn well better throw it. Else, that old man standing at home plate is gonna knock your ass so far off this here mound, you'll be in a vat of Emmett's Brunswick stew. You got that?"

"I'm the pitcher," argued Sonny Jim.

"And I'm fifty pounds bigger'n you, pissant."

Sonny Jim's face turned red. He knew Moody was at the point of madness. "All right," he mumbled. "Fastball."

Moody returned to his position behind home place. He stabbed a single finger toward the ground.

Sonny Jim nodded. He took his stance on the mound, checked Carver at second base, raised his arms, lowered them, paused, rocked against the pitching rubber, threw his leg up and around. He could feel the wind against his arm and the quick pain in his wrist as it snapped forward. He knew the ball had left precisely on command, knew it would gather speed over the distance, knew it would nip the inside edge of the plate, waist-high, tight against Monroe, close enough to put Monroe on alert that a Sonny Jim Wallace fastball had some danger about it.

Moody did not see Monroe's arms move. He reached for the ball and the ball was not there. He heard a sound like a deer rifle and he saw Sonny Jim's head jerk right, toward the left field line, watching the ball land three hundred and twenty feet away, rolling against the outfield fence. Moody lifted himself from his squatting position and Carver was on him, running easy, almost jogging, touching home plate with the tip of his toe. Moody was sure he heard Carver giggle.

"Damn," Moody muttered, spitting through his catcher's mask. He looked at Sonny Jim. Sonny Jim was glaring angrily at him. A chorus of boos rose lustily from the stands. Along the third base line, a few blacks applauded politely, their faces plastered in knowing smiles.

On the platform of the Coca-Cola scoreboard, Donnie Holbrook, the 12-year-old nephew of Seth Pennefeather, pulled metal numbers from a box and slipped them over hooks: Visitors 1, Home Team 0.

Monroe stood at first base, bent over, breathing hard, wheezing. He was waving for a timeout.

"Need my runner," Monroe said to Reece Baldwin, umpiring at first.

"Well, get him out here," said Reece.

Monroe waved toward the Bluejays' bench and a small boy, beautifully brown, emerged from the shoulders of the Bluejays' team. He ran quickly, easily across the infield and took his position at first.

"Wait a minute," Reece said to Monroe. "That boy's the runner?"

"He is," replied Monroe, smiling happily. "You stay close now," he instructed the boy. The boy nodded. He planted his left foot on first base and leaned forward, his hands propped against his knees.

A murmur of laughter filtered from the stands where the whites were sitting.

Inez said to Happy, "Look at that little boy. He's cute as a bug."

Happy said to Inez, "Inez, please shut up."

At first base, Reece asked, "How old is that boy?"

"He fourteen," answered Monroe.

"He could get hurt out here," warned Reece.

Monroe looked calmly at Reece. "That there's Junior Dawson. He my grandboy. All he's doing is running," he said.

"Well, just so you know," replied Reece. "We ain't responsible."

"That's right," said Monroe. "Don't expect nobody but me to be that." He winked at his grandson and walked away, faking a limp.

"Hey, Sonny Jim," Runt Ashford shouted from where he stood near the stands, "you better watch out, boy. You got you a se-mi-pro over there on first."

The crowd laughed lightly.

Sonny Jim rolled the ball in his hand. He circled the mound, looking toward first at Junior Dawson. Monroe must be a crazy man, he thought, putting a boy over on first. Apparently Monroe did not know about the famous Sonny Jim Wallace motion with a man on base. He dropped his head to cover his snicker.

Willie Fagin, the Bluejays' cleanup batter, stood patiently at the plate. Willie did not look like a baseball player. He was short and fat. His cap was twisted down on his ears, his baseball shirt pulled open between the buttons, his pants met his stockings above his knees. And he stood away from the plate on the back line of the batter's box, swinging a bat that looked like a two-by-four whittled down to a handle.

"Right down the middle, Sonny Jim," a partisan yelled.

"Don't worry, Sonny Jim. He gets a hit, it'll take a tow truck to get him down to first!"

Laughter grew from the stands. Willie turned in the direction of the voices and grinned. His hands squeezed on the bat.

Sonny Jim took his position on the mound and eyed Moody. One finger. Fastball. Sonny Jim cocked his head off his left shoulder, cutting his eyes to Junior Dawson. Junior lifted his foot from first base, took two small steps toward second, leaned forward at his waist. His arms were swinging free in front of him. He tapped the ground with the fingers of his right hand, as though testing it. Sonny Jim raised his arms above his head. His hands met in the prayer salute of the stretch motion. He dropped his hands slowly, made a head motion toward first. Junior stepped cautiously back toward the base and

Sonny Jim knew he had Junior intimidated. He snickered, rocked, kicked, whipped the ball into Moody's mitt.

A great roar erupted from the crowd and Sonny Jim whirled toward first. He did not see Junior. He turned quickly to second base. Junior was standing on the base, his hands resting on his hips. A calm, almost bored expression was on his face. Sonny Jim could not believe it. He mumbled, "Holy shit." He called to Reece, "Time!" Then he motioned for A.G. Tanner, who played first base for the Tigers. A.G. trotted to the mound, his eyes fixed in disbelief on Junior.

"What the hell happened?" demanded Sonny Jim in a hissing whisper.

A.G.'s face was pale. "I never saw nothing like that, Sonny Jim," he said, shaking his head. "He ain't hit the ground but three times from first to second. I swear to Jesus, he was three-quarters there before the ball got to Moody."

"Bullshit," Sonny Jim snapped, chewing on his lower lip. "He weren't but a foot off first."

"Yeah, well, you better look again," argued A.G. "I know where he *was* and I know where he *is,* and it ain't the same place. You better watch that little fart. He'll be halfway to Atlanta before you know it."

Clyde Mayberry stepped toward the mound from behind home plate. "Let's go, boys," he called to Sonny Jim and A.G. "Play ball."

A.G. turned and ambled back to first base. Sonny Jim glared at Junior, standing on top of second base. At home plate, Willie Fagin waited patiently, leaning on his bat like a man with a walking cane.

"We ain't got all day, Sonny Jim," yelled Clyde. "It's hot out here."

Sonny Jim climbed the mound, rooted his foot against the pitching rubber, fixed his stare on Willie. He called, "Where you want it, Tubs?" Willie raised his bat and flicked it easily across the heart of the plate. Moody squatted with his knees open. He dropped two fingers, then three. Sinker ball.

Sonny Jim twisted to look at Junior on second. Junior smiled and sat down on the base. The mockery of laughter from the stands stabbed at Sonny Jim. He hurried into his stretch motion, staring at Junior. Junior remained seated. Sonny Jim raised his arm, paused, then twisted back toward home plate. His arm came from straight overhead, like the swing of an ax. Two feet from the plate, the ball snapped downward and Willie whipped the bat in a graceful sweep. The ball rode four hundred and ten feet, dead center, clearing the fence by fifteen feet.

Donnie Holbrook scattered numbers on the platform of the Coca-Cola scoreboard, changing the score: Visitors 3, Home Team 0. One out. Top of the first.

Elmo's face was splotched in shock and anger. He grabbed a bat and slammed it against the ground. The bat broke in a clean snap. "Time!" he bellowed to Clyde Mayberry. He marched across the infield to the mound, still holding the broken stub of the bat.

In the stands, Runt Ashford said aloud, "Damn. Elmo's gonna kill Sonny Jim."

Sonny Jim stood on the mound, quivering. He could see Elmo's lips tightening in hard white streaks. He saw Elmo's vice-grip on the broken bat.

"Ah—what you gonna do with that bat, Elmo?" Sonny Jim asked timidly, glancing toward A.G. at first base.

"Cram it up somebody's ass, splinters first," Elmo growled in a low voice, "if that somebody don't start throwing some outs. I'm not letting no colored team beat me, you hear that, Sonny Jim?"

"I hear that, Elmo."

Elmo thrust his face close to Sonny Jim's face. "You believe what I'm saying, Sonny Jim?"

"I believe it, Elmo."

"You better, by God, or you gonna be a walking piece of stovewood."

Elmo turned quickly and stalked away.

"Come on, boys!" a hefty, red-faced woman screamed from the bottom row of the stands. "Look alive."

Near her, Runt Ashford could feel the boiling of anger in his chest. He muttered, "It ain't right. It ain't right."

On the mound, Sonny Jim had listened well to Elmo's warning. He got the next two batters for the Bluejays to pop up in the infield.

A cry of relief, lathered with nervous applause, rolled down from the stands.

The man who always pitched the first three innings for the Bluejays—before Washington Doubletree made his celebrated appearance in the fourth inning—was Truman Hill, called Birdman by his teammates. Truman was the color of rich, black ink. He was tall and skinny. His arms flopped humorously at his sides, like a puppet's arms. His feet look hinged in the middle. He called his feet his Cadillacs—"streamlined and made for moving." Truman was not a baseball player of great distinction. He was, in fact, a clown, a comic relief used by Monroe to lull the opposition into overconfidence before Washington assumed command. If Truman could not distract a hitter by his motion, or the improvised dance he performed on the mound, he resorted to his specialty—birdcalls. Truman Hill could imitate anything with wings. It was a joke in Jefferson that he had once managed to drive a redbird and a hawk into crossbreeding by whistling out of both sides of his mouth at the same time during mating season.

And Truman was the pitcher for the Bluejays in the first inning of the first Annual Founders Day semi-professional baseball game. Warming up, he entertained. He danced. He made birdcalls. He smiled. He doffed his cap. Applause rained down on him. And laughter. He threw four pitches, easy lobs, to Monroe, who was seated comfortably on his stool behind home plate, and then he called, "Batter up. Birdman's ready to go." He did a shrill cry of an eagle diving for some unsuspecting prey burrowed in field grass. He tapped the pitching rubber in a light soft-shoe step, and then he ceremoniously removed his cap and smiled broadly for the crowd. A hoot erupted from the stands.

"Go get that smart-ass," Elmo commanded A.G. Tanner, who was the leadoff hitter for the Tigers.

A.G. paraded to the batter's box. He pounded home plate with his bat, cocked his elbows in a dramatic pose, positioned his feet, pushed his butt backward, bent his knees.

Truman backed off the mound, cupped his hand over his cap to receive the sign from Monroe. One finger. Fastball. A fastball was the only pitch Truman could throw, yet he insisted Monroe flash a sign. Any sign. To Truman, even a clown deserved some dignity.

Truman's windup looked like a seizure in a religious experience featuring rapture. It tied his arms and legs into a knot, then untied them in a herky-jerky motion that gave the appearance of coming unhinged from the trunk of his body.

His first pitch was a ball, high against A.G.'s chest. A.G. smiled. He heard Elmo's icy instruction from the bench: "Hit him!"

Truman's next pitch was waist high, across the middle of the plate. A.G. slapped it over third base, a foot inside the line. The ball skittered for a double.

A roar exploded from the stands.

"We got 'em now," someone bellowed.

And they were right. Before Truman managed to retire the side, the score was 5-3, Tigers.

"That's more like it," Elmo muttered.

The Bluejays added a run in the second inning, narrowing the score to 5-4. Truman bird called and danced his way to a scoreless bottom of the second, and Sonny Jim matched him in the top of the third. And then Truman returned to pitch his last inning. Elmo knew the Tigers would have to score against Truman. Truman was a clown; Washington Doubletree was not. He called his team into a huddle as Truman toyed with his warm-up pitches.

"All right," Elmo lectured in a low, mean voice, "this is how it is: you got a quota. This inning, by God, I better see me some hitting and running and scoring. I better see me at least three runs, or they's gonna be hell to pay."

It was a brief, though inspirational message. No one enjoyed paying Elmo's hell. The Tigers scored four runs on five hits, including three consecutive doubles, before Truman managed to retire Billy Bolingbroke for the third out. The scoreboard read 9-4, Tigers.

Elmo permitted a pleased and private snarl. His team knew him well, he thought.

In the stands, fans of the Tigers—the whites—jabbered in gladness, jittery with energy. Along the third base line, and on the knoll behind the outfield fence, the blacks that had gathered to watch the game, nodded and smiled. They were enjoying the antics of Truman Hill, who had left the mound gleefully, stopping halfway in the infield and removing his cap in a grand sweep of his arm. He bowed graciously to the crowd, like a Shakespearean actor. The crowd laughed hysterically. The crowd pointed and hooted. Truman was center stage and he knew it. He picked up a ball that Monroe had rolled back across the infield and began to toss it in the air. He then held it high on the tip of his fingers and walked in a slow, dragging dance step to Washington Doubletree and bowed again. He handed Washington the ball in a comic demonstration of surrender. Washington folded the ball into his hand and the ball completely disappeared.

"Godalmighty," Sonny Jim whispered to Moody. "You see that?"

The Bluejays were suddenly a different team. They sat forward on the edge of their players' benches and began a musical chatter of encouragement. Truman was their leader. He pranced before the bench like a drum major, clapping his hands in an easy rhythm, whistling, begging performance from his teammates.

Along the third base line and on the knoll behind the outfield fence, black fans picked up Truman's handclap, turning it into a sound of joy. A few whites joined in.

It was Saturday afternoon, April 9, 1955, in Claybank, Georgia. Founders (with no apostrophe) Day. It was hot. The smell of Emmett Mulherne's barbecue slithered across space. The greatest baseball game in the history of north Georgia was being played, and it was about to become legendary.

"Batter up!" Clyde Mayberry shouted. "Let's play ball."

Monroe Dawson, sitting quietly on his catcher's stool at the end of the Bluejays' bench, raised his hand and Truman abruptly stopped his show. Monroe looked down the bench. Every man on his team held his gaze. He nodded once.

For three innings the Bluejays had played cautiously, with a deceiving reserve. Junior Dawson's steal of second and Willie Fagin's distant home run had been awesome feats, but the Bluejays had relaxed after Truman started pitching, as though Truman's unpredictable behavior was more enjoyable than the game.

Now it was the top of the fourth inning and the Bluejays were trailing by four runs. Alfred Oldfield walked to the plate.

"Hey, when y'all gonna start playing some ball?" Moody said in a derisive tone to Alfred. "In case you can't add that high, we up by five runs." Moody giggled at his own humor.

Alfred stared blankly at Moody. "Monroe say we start now," he said.

A chill raced across Moody's shoulders.

The Bluejays scored five runs with the precision of a military drill team in a parade. Sonny Jim was stunned, battle-shocked. His neck hurt from watching the ball flash by him, deftly guided to an empty spot on the field. The score was tied, 9-9, and Elmo had had enough. He yelled to Clyde Mayberry for a time-out and then he marched to the mound.

"Sonny Jim," Elmo said, yanking the ball away from Sonny Jim's trembling hand, "problem with you is you ain't got no guts. You a candy-ass."

"What's that mean, Elmo?" whimpered Sonny Jim. "I ain't no candy-ass."

"You letting them colored boys knock your teeth down your throat, ain't you? That's candy-ass. You had any guts, you'd be throwing between their eyes, make them hang back. But you ain't doing that, so you can take your candy-ass off this field and find you a place on the bench, or go home and take up knitting."

"Who's gonna pitch, Elmo?" asked Sonny Jim. "We got nobody warmed up."

Elmo's eyes narrowed. He glared at Sonny Jim. "Me," he said. He grabbed Sonny Jim's glove and turned to the mound.

"Elmo—"

"Sonny Jim, I don't like candy-asses," Elmo hissed in a whisper. "I ain't pitched in years, but I can out-throw anybody we got." He motioned to Clyde, indicating that he was removing Sonny Jim and inserting himself into the lineup. The crowd fell silent. Elmo had never played a minute of baseball since becoming manager of the Tigers.

Clyde strolled to the mound.

"What's going on, Elmo?" he asked.

"I'm putting Candy-Ass Sonny Jim over on the bench," Elmo said, "and I'm taking his place."

"You?"

"Me."

"You can't play, Elmo. You ain't on the roster," Clyde said.

"The hell, I ain't. Look where it says Manager," Elmo snapped.

Clyde's face furrowed in confusion. "I think that stretches the meaning of what a roster is," he suggested. "Just a tad, I mean. Not sure what Monroe will think about it."

"We bent some rules for him. Tell him we bending a few more," Elmo ordered.

Clyde wagged his head and walked away, toward Monroe. The rulebook as he knew it had already been amended to a league of cow pasture baseball. Another twist wouldn't matter much. Besides, Elmo was right; concessions had been made for Monroe. Wasn't much Monroe could complain about.

"We got us a little situation," he said to Monroe. He turned back to look at Elmo, who was standing on the mound, talking to Moody.

"It's all right," Monroe told him. "Let him play. Been hearing about him for years, but never seen him play."

"I appreciate the understanding," Clyde said.

A buzz of voices hummed in the stands and up and down the first base line. Runt Ashford tapped a cigarette from its package and lit it. An anxious expression was etched in his face.

"What's he doing?" Darby Robinson asked Runt. Darby owned a sawmill and was considered the strongest man in Claybank County.

"Damned if I know," Runt answered. "But I can tell you this: it'd better work. He lets them niggers win this game, he's gonna wish he never was born."

Elmo warmed up easily. His tall, lean body obeyed the rehearsal of younger years and he began to throw harder with each pitch. After ten pitches, he signaled to Clyde Mayberry that he was ready.

Clyde leaned over home plate to brush it off with a whiskbroom he carried in his hip pocket. He whispered to Moody, "What's he got?"

"He's fast," Moody said. "My hand's already burning."

Clyde stood erect and motioned to Elmo. He called, "You sure you ready?" The question was for the benefit of the crowd.

"I'm ready," Elmo answered coldly.

The first Bluejay to face Elmo was King Whitley, who played third base. King was the only left-handed batter on the Bluejays' team and Elmo had a special disregard for left-handers.

The first pitch Elmo threw was straight at King's mouth. King flicked his head and the ball sailed past Moody. The crowd oohed. Monroe slipped forward on his stool by the Bluejays' bench. His face was furrowed.

The second pitch missed King by an inch and knocked Moody backward. Mumbling began in the crowd. The men on the Bluejays' bench began whispering among themselves.

The third pitch was a round-house curve that King slapped to Felton Simpson at third base. Felton threw to A.G. at first. One out.

Truman Hill was the next batter. He shouldered his bat and started toward home plate, staring contemptuously at Elmo. Monroe's voice stopped him.

"Birdman," Monroe said sharply.

Truman turned and walked back to the bench. A smile rode across his face. Monroe nodded to Washington Doubletree. Washington pulled a dark, heavy bat from beneath the bench and crossed to home plate in a slow walk.

"Wait a minute," Elmo protested from the mound. "Washington's not supposed to play before the fourth inning."

Monroe stood quickly at his stool. He no longer seemed to be an old man. "Not supposed to *pitch* before the fourth," he corrected in a stern voice. He sat again.

Elmo stalked the mound, kicking at the pitching rubber, silently cursing. Monroe had him, and he knew it. Even rules that had enough bend in them to look like pretzels demanded respect. Besides, if he threw a fit, things could get nasty, especially with people like Runt Ashford and his crowd in the stands. He rolled his shoulders and the fire of pain burned in his muscles. His ruined elbow throbbed.

"Play ball!" Clyde thundered.

Elmo placed his right foot firmly against the pitching rubber. He glared at Washington Doubletree at home plate. Washington was a giant. He stood erect, holding the bat in his right hand, across his right shoulder, his left hand dangling by his side.

"You gonna hit that way?" asked Clyde.

Washington did not reply. He turned his head to stare at Clyde. The look was cold, a dare. Clyde leaned into his position behind Moody. He muttered, "I don't give a shit. Hit the way you want to."

On the mound, Elmo fixed his gaze on Moody. He flicked his head to the right, almost imperceptibly, yet Moody understood the signal. Fastball, up and in. He moved his mitt close to Washington's body and jabbed one finger toward the ground. Elmo nodded and began his motion. Anger boiled in him. Sidearmed, he thought. Throw it sidearmed. Sling it. That'd get the bastard moving.

The ball came in a blur from below Elmo's waist, sighing in the still, humid air. It began to rise as it approached Washington, headed for his neck. Washington did not move. His left hand flew up from his side and he caught the ball in his bare fist, like swiping a fly in midair.

Voices rang out from the stands.

"Oooooooh!"

"My God!"

"Jee-sus H. Christ!"

The voices were of awe, of disbelief, of fear.

Elmo stood frozen in his follow-through. His eyes widened as he stared at Washington holding the ball. He knew he had never thrown a ball as fast, not even in his youth, before his injury, and Washington Doubletree had caught it with his bare hand without flinching. And he had never seen a man's face as calm as Washington's face, Washington telling him with his eyes that he would not be intimidated and would not surrender. Washington rolled the ball around in his left hand, squeezing it with his fingers. He then flipped the ball to Moody, who had fallen back against Clyde.

"Hit batsman," Clyde called. "Take your base."

"Didn't hit me," said Washington. "I caught it."

Clyde removed his facemask and wiped perspiration from his face. The game he had agreed to umpire for Founders Day had become a mockery of baseball, no different than a game of Jacks-are-wild poker. "Fine with me," he said. "This whole thing's a joke anyway. Ball one."

Sitting beside the Bluejays' bench, Monroe smiled and rubbed his aching legs.

Elmo did not argue Clyde's confused call. He wanted to pitch to Washington, but he had lost his passion for mayhem. He walked Washington on three more wild pitches. His body cried from the unbearable ache of pain. He knew he could not throw in anger. He knew he had to rely on leftover skills that had made him a major league prospect.

Once.

Long ago.

Placement, Elmo thought. Picking at corners. Change of speed. Disguised motions on the mound.

His mind began to narrow on the plate. Sounds of the crowd faded into echoes. He began to think of his arm as it had been as a young man and for a moment—from the magic of memory—his arm was healed. It stayed healed for two more batters, both grounding out to A.G. at first base.

The patrons of the First Annual Founders Day Semi-Professional Baseball Game had lost their sense of propriety. They were becoming frenzied in the steaming afternoon heat and Washington Doubletree's feat—his very appearance—had left them anxious and rumbling.

Otha Estes could feel the building of tension. He stood a few feet from Runt, blocked by a gathering of men who had been drinking and were tightening into a knot of bravery. The men were listening to Runt swear vengeance on Washington, calling him an ". . . uppity damn nigger." Echoes of agreement came from the men.

Otha moved away to search for Compton Kent and Charles Doeman. He would need his deputies if things got ugly.

It was the bottom of the fourth inning. Washington Doubletree stood motionless on the mound, a great, black statue. He did not take warm-up pitches. He waited until Monroe had pushed the legs of his stool firmly into the ground and Felton Simpson had moved hesitantly to home plate as the Tigers' first batter. Felton had never seen Washington pitch, but he had heard the stories. Felton's knees trembled. His mouth was dry. His hands were slippery with perspiration.

"Tell me when he's ready," Clyde said to Monroe at home plate.

"He ready," Monroe answered.

"He ain't gonna throw no warm-ups?"

"He don't need none," Monroe replied.

Clyde shook his head. "This is the craziest damn ball game ever played anywhere in the world," he mumbled. He jerked his facemask over his face and waved to Washington.

Washington stepped to the pitching rubber, standing erect, with both feet together. He lifted the fall from his glove and presented it for Felton to see. He then closed his hand around the ball, and the ball disappeared as though swallowed by some prehistoric tentacled mouth. He bowed slightly and then began his motion. Felton was mesmerized. He heard a high, off-key whine and a sickening explosion behind him as the ball buried into Monroe's mitt. He heard Monroe's hurting moan and Clyde Mayberry's shaking voice as he called a strike.

The crowd fell silent.

"Lordy," Monroe complained in a low voice, "he gonna break this old man's hand."

"Monroe, you damn well better not miss that thing," whispered Clyde. "I ain't insured for this."

Washington struck out Felton on two more pitches and then struck out Dennis Albright on three pitches. Neither Felton nor Dennis had moved the bat from the shoulders. Neither had moved, not even to offer the customary swings before the pitch. They had stood immobile, horrified, unable to react to the execution before them. Jack Conway approached the plate hesitantly, barely hearing the counsel of the crowd: *"Swing the bat, Jack! You got to swing the bat!"* Jack did swing the bat. Three times. Feebly. And always late. Washington Doubletree had thrown nine pitches and had retired the side.

The fans that were black—the Bluejays' partisans—applauded Washington's performance exuberantly. The whites sat in shock.

"Look at him," Runt seethed, pointing at Washington. "Nothing on earth worse than a smart-aleck nigger."

"That's the truth," said a man standing beside Runt.

"You can say that again," offered another man.

Runt elbowed his way to the front of the crowd. He pushed himself up on tiptoes and covered his forehead with the palm of his hand and glared across the field to a congregation of blacks standing outside the third base line.

"Look over there, Darby" Runt said sarcastically "Looks like that's your nigger, Claude, laughing his ass off." He pointed with his hand, jabbing the air. "I don't care if he does work for you down there at the sawmill, you better get over there and tell him to keep shut or he's gonna get his ass handed to him on the barrel of a twelve-gauge."

Darby Robinson stepped forward, beside Runt, dwarfing him. "Uh-huh," he said, "that's Claude." He waved to Claude and Claude waved back in a timid half-gesture.

"I tell you what, Runt," Darby added easily. "Old Claude's been working for me for fifteen years. Best man I ever had. You just think about touching one kink of the hair on his head and I'm gonna split you like a piece of stovewood." He turned to the men with Runt and smiled pleasantly. "And that goes for any man out here," he said.

A beat of silence fell over the men, then one of them said, "Claude ain't doing nothing far as I can see."

On the field, the game of Happy Colquitt's dream, the game to increase business for Founders Day in Claybank, was no longer a game. It was war. Happy laughed gleefully in his special seat in the roped-off celebrity section of the bleachers. He reached across Inez to pull at Seth Pennefeather's arm. "Told you," Happy bragged. "Told you, didn't I? Huh? Didn't I?"

"You did," agreed Seth. "You did. It's nice, real nice."

Elmo knew he was lying to his arm, telling it the year was 1947, telling it there was no pain, no burning ache. Yet he knew he had to lie. He could not break down before Washington Doubletree. In some way that he understood but could not explain, he was inextricably bound to his great black foe, and his great black foe was inextricably bound to him. He had never seen an athlete the equal of Washington Doubletree. Never. He did not believe he could defeat Washington, but he could not break. And then he realized the truth—the blinding *déjà vu* truth. He was in the game that all athletes know in premonition; he was in his final game, and it had a value as important as death well earned.

The arm heard Elmo's lie, told with such purring deception that the arm believed. It worked from memory, bravely, defiantly, short-circuiting the punishment of swelling muscle and ripped nerves. Through the fifth and sixth innings, Elmo retired the Bluejays with only two wasted singles—one by Washington and one by Mizell Cofer. But Washington was flawless, striking out each man he faced. Nine strikeouts in a row. Score tied, 9-9.

In the top of the seventh, Willie Fagin powered his second home run to give the Bluejays a 10-9 lead, and the followers of the Claybank Textile Tigers could sense the doom of defeat. The crowd cried for courage. Their cries were aimed at Elmo and Elmo's suffering.

"Com'on, Elmo!"

"Hold 'em, Elmo!"

"Get it back, Elmo!"

Happy's joy of the game had soured. The Bluejays were winning and Elmo was hurting.

"What's the matter, Happy, honey?" asked Inez.

"Nothing," Happy snarled. "I got to go down and get some pictures."

"You want me to go with you?"

"Good God, no, Inez. You just stay right here, next to Seth. If I don't see you after the game, I'll see you at the barbecue."

Inez smiled. She was hot and tired. The game was of no interest to her. She said to Happy, "I may just go on home. The sun's really getting to me."

Happy shrugged. He eased his way in front of Inez and Seth and Whitman Robart. At the end of the bleacher, Ralph Claybank caught his arm and pulled at it. He leaned to listen.

"Elmo looks like he's dying," Ralph said frantically. "Poor boy looks like he can't stand up."

Happy could smell a thick musk aftershave lotion on Ralph's neck. "Well, yeah, he's getting his ass kicked," he said to Ralph.

"He's doing it all wrong," Ralph said excitedly. "Raybert—" He motioned with his head to the tall, muscular, suntanned man sitting beside him. "Raybert said he should have our lads put their bats right out in front of that big mitt that old black man's wearing and just let the bat hit the ball."

"Well, Raybert's not out there," Happy said defensively. "And I'd guess Elmo knows a little bit more about the game than Raybert does."

Ralph's face blushed red in anger. "You don't have to take that tone, Happy," he said curtly. "I'll have you know that Raybert used to play baseball."

Happy shot a surprised look at Raybert and Raybert smiled and nodded a yes. "In New York," he said.

My God, Happy thought.

"So, maybe Raybert knows something that Elmo doesn't know," argued Ralph.

"Maybe so," Happy replied. "And maybe you ought to go tell Elmo what he's doing wrong. I got newspaper work to do." He turned and pushed his way to the end of the bleachers.

"Maybe I will," Ralph called out angrily. "That's exactly what I'll do. It's my team." He stood and maneuvered his way through the crowd, then walked past Runt and Darby and the crowd of men standing behind the hogwire backstop.

"Godamighty," Runt snorted. "Where the hell he think he's going?"

"Headed toward Elmo," someone answered.

"Maybe Elmo can put him in the game," Runt said. "We need a swish-hitter."

The men around Runt roared with laughter.

"Go get 'em, Ralph," a voice chortled.

"Kick ass, Ralph," someone else called.

Elmo could see Ralph approaching the bench. He dropped his head and whispered, "Jesus." He could feel the blood of embarrassment flood into his face.

"Elmo, Elmo," Ralph said, pushing onto the bench next to Elmo.

"What you doing down here?" Elmo demanded.

A look of surprise, then hurt, flashed in Ralph's eyes. He said, "Why, Elmo, I own the team. I can come down here if I want to. My daddy used to sit on the bench with the fellows all the time."

Elmo moved his face close to Ralph and growled in a low voice: "Well, you ain't your daddy, and this ain't the time or the place to start acting like him."

"Now, you stop it," Ralph said in a stern voice. "I'm just here to help."

"Help?" Elmo exclaimed. Perspiration rolled from his face. He rubbed his numbing arm. "What in the name of God are you talking about?"

"My friend Raybert said all you had to do was put the bat in front of that big mitt, or catcher's glove, or whatever you call it. Raybert said that big black fellow was just throwing the ball to it— the mitt, or whatever it is."

"Well, damn, Ralph, I know that," Elmo said wearily. "He ain't just throwing at it, he's hitting it dead center."

"Precisely."

"Precisely? What the hell does that mean?"

Ralph smiled triumphantly. "It means you let the ball hit the bat, instead of trying to make the bat hit the ball."

Elmo shook his head in disbelief. He picked up a towel and wiped it across his face. He could hear laughter from Runt and Runt's followers. He could smell Emmett Mulherne's barbecue in the hot spring air. His arm throbbed.

"Ralph," Elmo said quietly, "tell you what: if you go back to where you was and leave me alone, I'll do what you said."

"Good," Ralph replied. "That's what I like. Cooperation." He patted Elmo's hurting arm. "You tell our lads I'm proud of them." He stood and marched away to the cheers of Runt and Runt's followers.

Elmo sat alone, his head lowered, staring at the ground. Ralph had just touched him. Ralph had been sitting on the bench reserved for athletes. Ralph had offered him advice. He looked across the infield at Washington Doubletree standing patiently on the pitcher's mound as the Bluejays' infielders played their catch-and-throw warm-ups. It stunned Elmo that Washington did not warm up, yet he also knew there was no reason for it; it would be a waste of energy. Watching Washington was like watching a magnificent warrior from some battle out of history. He was imposing, his game flawless.

Or was it?

Elmo stretched his shoulder muscles against his uniform. Maybe not, he thought. Maybe Washington had an Achilles heel that nobody had ever seen, a pinhole soft spot in the armor of his awesome talent. Maybe Ralph Claybank was right—or his friend, Raybert. Maybe if the Tigers stood at the plate and only pretended to watch Washington, but kept their eyes cheating to Monroe's placement of the mitt and then, when Washington began his windup, if they dropped their bats over the mitt, like a bar across a gate, then maybe, just maybe, they could bunt themselves on base. The way Washington came off the mound was awkward, more like a lumbering rhinoceros than a graceful lion. Fielding a bunt would not be easy for him.

"Who's up?" Elmo asked Joe Eberhard, the Tigers' lineup keeper.

"Felton," Joe said.

Elmo moved from the bench. He walked over to Felton and folded his left arm around Felton's shoulder and whispered into Felton's ear. Felton stepped back and looked at Elmo in shock. Elmo took the bat from Felton's hands and gave him a quick, covered instruction. Felton nodded. The nod said, "I'll try."

Elmo returned to the bench and sat beside Joe Eberhard.

"What'd you tell him?" asked Joe.

Elmo did not answer. He hugged his aching right arm with his left hand. He turned and looked quickly in the bleachers. He could see Ralph Claybank talking with his friend, Raybert, and suddenly his memory flashed: Raybert—Ray—Pennyworth. Centerfielder for the New York Giants in the late years of the war. Hit in the face by a rookie pitcher from the Dodgers, blinding him in one eye, ending his career. Ray Pennyworth. The son of a bitch could play baseball. It was disgusting seeing him with Ralph.

From the field, Clyde Mayberry called, "Play ball!"

In the batter's box, Felton stood deep as commanded by Elmo. Close to the plate, open stance. His bat was short-cocked by his ear. His head was turned slightly in Monroe's direction. He glanced at Washington as Washington presented the ball, drew it in, engulfed it in his hand, rocked and threw.

Felton timed the motion perfectly. He slipped the bat down over the mouth of Monroe's mitt, squeezing the handle tight in his hands. His hands felt the concussion of the ball before Felton realized he had hit it. The ball ricocheted hard into the ground toward third base, spinning wildly. Felton dropped his bat and started his dash toward first base. He could see Washington freeze at the foot of the mound, watching the ball skitter across the infield. He crossed first base before Washington could reach the ball.

"Godalmighty!" Runt shouted, and the crowd around him exploded in a piercing cheer.

A surge of adrenaline, electric in intensity, shot through Elmo. He turned to look at Ralph. Ralph was standing, applauding. He flipped a wave toward Elmo, then began hugging himself with gladness. He did a joyful pirouette with his arms extended above his head and embraced Raybert shamelessly. My God, Elmo thought, that's just plain disgusting.

Felton's bunt single renewed the spirits, and the skills, of the Tigers. Following Elmo's instruction, Dennis Albright and Jack Conway followed in a parade of offense. Three consecutive bunts. The Bluejays were off stride by the strategy. No one had ever bunted against Washington. No one had ever wanted to risk death by getting that close to the ball. Still, the bases were loaded and no outs had been recorded.

At the Tigers' bench, Elmo paced nervously. He watched as Monroe called for a time-out to talk to Washington. Whatever was said was said by Monroe. Washington only listened and nodded. Elmo guessed Monroe had warned of a squeeze play. The set up was perfect, too perfect to resist, especially with the clumsy way Washington fielded bunts and with Monroe sitting on a stool behind home plate. Monroe would never get off his stool fast enough to cover home plate on a squeeze play. He was too old, too slow.

Elmo laced his fingers together and held them in front of his chest, flashing the squeeze play sign to Sammy Atkinson, who was coaching at third base. Sammy's hands danced over his body, like a man picking fleas, translating Elmo's order to Felton at third base and to Jasper Turner, who stood at home plate. Felton stepped off third and took three steps toward home.

On the mound, Washington Doubletree's face betrayed him. He no longer had the look of solemnity, the dreaded stone expression. His eyes twitched. He licked his lips. A coating of perspiration glistened from his forehead. His mind worked in replay. He could see the falling, dying trickery of the ball rolling toward him, mocking the awkwardness of his follow-through. Yet, he had to have the follow-through; it was the secret of his speed. He stood staring at Jasper Turner. Jasper was back in the box, his stance open, his bat short-cocked at his ear. It would be another bunt—the squeeze play, where the runner at third would be running on the pitch, challenging whoever fielded the ball to get it to the catcher in time for the out. He hoped Monroe knew what he was doing.

Behind the plate, Monroe moved his mitt inside and Jasper saw the motion. He dropped his bat to cover the mitt. Monroe moved the mitt again, farther inside. Jasper began to quiver. If Washington missed by a half-inch, Jasper knew he would have a hole in him three inches wide. Washington saw Monroe's right hand squeeze twice and he knew what Monroe wanted him to do. He began his motion.

The pitch did not sing against the wind. It floated. Lazy. Soft. Jasper's right hand slid up the handle of the bat, leveling it. From the corner of his eye, he saw Felton in a sprint toward home plate. The ball was hanging, dropping in a slow arch, and Jasper knew instantly what had happened: Monroe had called for a fool pitch—one bounce into his mitt and he would simply reach out and touch Felton before Felton could reach home plate. Jasper lunged for the ball. His bat tapped it just before it hit the ground in front of home plate. The ball rolled slowly toward the mound and Jasper stumbled for first base, crawl-running on his hands and toes. Monroe tried to push himself off the stool, but he was too late. Felton's slide bulled into him and he fell heavily, yet he did not take his eyes from the ball. He saw Washington's recovery from the half-follow of his pitch and he saw Jasper's off-balance, stumbling race down the first base line.

146

Washington fielded the ball with his bare hand and threw it to Alfred Oldfield at first. A run had scored, but Jasper was out.

The score was 10-10 and Otha Estes had his hand on the handle of his holstered pistol. Felton's slide into Monroe had caused the players of both teams to leap from their benches. Otha knew temper. It was not a fight between the teams that bothered him; it was the fuse of a riot. He stepped close to Runt as Runt began to move for the field.

"Runt," Otha growled, "you even think about going out there and I'll slap you to kingdom come and then I'll kick your ass."

Runt stopped in mid-step and glared at Otha.

"Runt's not going nowhere, Otha," Darby Robinson said. "He's just trying to get a better look, him being not much bigger than a midget. Ain't that right, Runt?"

A look of pain shot across Runt's face. He crossed his arms and looked down and pawed at the ground with the tip of his shoe.

"Runt's fine," Darby said gently.

On the field, Clyde Mayberry and Felton and Elmo were the first to reach Monroe, who was holding his left side and gasping for breath. The players of both teams stood at their benches and waited for the hot moment of a riot to happen.

"You all right, Monroe?" Clyde asked anxiously, helping Monroe to his knees. Monroe nodded.

"Where you hurting?" Elmo asked.

Monroe smiled painfully. "All over, but my pride more'n anything," he answered in a soft voice. He looked up at Felton. "Son, a few years ago, I'd of been clear out of the way."

Felton grinned. "Yessir," he said. "I expect you would have."

Elmo and Clyde half-lifted Monroe to his feet. The teams sat at their benches. The crowd applauded appreciatively in relief.

"You gonna keep playing?" Elmo asked.

147

Monroe rubbed his face with the sleeve of his uniform. He lifted his left arm and rotated it to exercise the muscles. He said to Elmo, "Somebody told me you was from Cuttercane."

"I am," Elmo replied. "Why?"

"Where I'm from, too," Monroe said. "Long time ago. Long time before you was born."

"I'll be damned," Elmo replied in surprise.

"You get dunked in Asa's Spring?" Monroe asked.

"I did," Elmo told him.

"Me, too," Monroe said quietly. "My daddy sneaked me in there one night when no white folks was around. They was them that thought I had the polio. Don't know what it was, but I come out a baseball player." He slapped dirt from his mitt. "Wonder what them folks would be thinking about us right along now?" he added. "Two old Cuttercane boys dunked in Asa's Spring, going at it." He looked at Elmo and the flicker of a young smile played across his cracked lips. "Am I gonna keep playing? Yes, sir. We can't quit. Not me. Not you. No sir, we can't. We been dunked in Asa's Spring. We got to keep playing." He chuckled and began to limp toward the mound, motioning for Washington Doubletree.

Elmo watched as Monroe talked to Washington in a low voice, and he knew the game was about to change. Monroe would not be beaten by a high school stunt, and Ralph's advice—though it had worked temporarily—was a high school stunt.

Monroe returned to home plate and positioned himself on his stool. Moody Hickman waited to bat for the Tigers.

"You all right?" asked Moody.

"Good as a old man can be," replied Monroe. "You boys got us on the run. Yessir, you have."

"Let's play ball," Clyde said from behind Monroe.

Moody stepped into the batter's box, dug his spikes into the hard red clay. He tilted his head toward Washington, but kept his eyes cast down, cutting them toward Monroe. Monroe pushed his mitt up, held it for a quick moment, then dropped it. He pushed it up a second time, but in a difference position, then dropped it again. Pushed it up, again in a different position. He then dropped it between his legs, letting it dangle free. Moody was confused. He glanced toward the mound. Washington was turning to face second base, his back to home plate.

"What the hell—?" Moody mumbled in confusion.

Washington gazed at Jack Conway at second. He raised his shoulders in his erect, military posture and presented the ball to Jack as though Jack was the batter. He then began his methodical windup.

At home plate, Moody watched nervously. Washington would have to twirl on the mound to throw toward home plate and that would be the same as throwing blind. A bolt of fear shot through Moody. Jesus, he thought, he could kill me throwing that way. He could bust my skull. His brain told him to move, but it was too late. Washington's body was twisting toward him like a thing of unleashed vengeance. Moody was mesmerized. He did not see Monroe's mitt flash into place, exactly where it had been on Monroe's third positioning. He heard the explosion of ball burying into Monroe's mitt and Clyde's bellowing call, "Striiiiiiike!"

Elmo's shoulders sagged. He knew what Monroe was doing, and he knew he had no answer for it. Monroe had coded the placement of the ball and Washington had memorized the placement before turning his back. Washington was not throwing to a mitt; he was throwing to a mind picture. The act of facing second base was a circus trick, a show-off move to send a message of intimidation. And it worked. Washington struck out Moody and Billy Bolingbroke on six pitches.

On the mound, Elmo's arm was burning. His fingers tingled. He begged his mind for the barrier to break, for the after-pain sensation of no feeling. He had known men who were able to withstand pain, whose bodies slipped into shock and functioned only on discipline.

But the pain would not leave and Elmo's arm began convulsing between pitches. He could not snap his wrist. He could not guide the ball. Still, he could not quit.

The Bluejays scored one run in the eighth inning when Monroe singled with Alfred Oldfield on second base. Washington then retired the Tigers with three strikeouts in the bottom of the eighth inning. Donnie Holbrook posted the score: Visitors 11, Home 10.

In the stands, jubilation turned to restlessness and the hooting sound of boos rang across the field. Runt Ashford's voice promised threat.

In the top of the ninth, Elmo's luck held. He retired the Bluejays on two fly-outs and an infield dribbler, and the voice of the fans became desperate. One more turn at bat for Tigers. One last chance to win a game that had become brutal in its intensity.

"Com'on, Tigers, you can do it!"

"Com'on, babe! Com'on, boy!"

"Don't take but one to tie, two to win!"

"Don't let us down!"

And Clyde Mayberry heard the anguish of Tiger fans whining for a miracle that did not seem possible. Was not possible. Not without his influence. He had promised impartiality as an umpire, but he knew what his life would be like in weeks to come if he did not offer a helping hand, or a blind eye, to the cause of the Tigers.

Clyde called two walks against Washington, one on a 3-2 count and the other on a 3-1 count. Every pitch had been a strike.

Along the third base line and on the knoll beyond the outfield fence, followers of the Bluejays began to stir, to mutter objections to Clyde's favoritism. Frowns plowed across the faces of Otha Estes and Happy Colquitt. The presence of trouble was like the tremor of a distant earthquake.

Behind home plate, Monroe sensed the tremor. He saw the jittery foot dancing of the Bluejay fans down the third base line. He pulled himself from his stool and stood wearily, his head bent, his hands propped on his hips. Then he raised his hand and called for a time-out.

"Don't go stalling, Monroe," Clyde Mayberry advised in a voice intended for the nearby fans.

"No sir," Monroe said softly. He made a slight throwing motion toward Washington with his right arm. "Better throw the hard stuff now," he called.

"What you talking about?" Clyde asked suspiciously.

"He been holding back," Monroe said. "Hit the umpire a couple of weeks ago. Eddie Doss. Maybe you run across him somewhere. I hear tell he moved back in with his mama when they let him out of the hospital last week. Don't know how it happened. Just got by me. He been holding back ever since." He paused, wiped the perspiration from his forehead with his sleeve. "But it look like he's turned wild, don't it? Way he walking everybody. But don't you worry none, Mr. Mayberry. I'll do my best to not let nothing get past me this time. No sir. " He chuckled and pulled the catcher's mask over his face. "Anyhow, I got a feeling he's gonna start throwing strikes."

Clyde stared at Monroe. His face turned pale.

"You ready to finish this game?" Monroe asked.

Clyde nodded.

Washington struck out A.G. Tanner on three pitches.

"He looking better," Monroe said to Clyde. "Yessir, looks like his old self."

The last two outs were quick and orderly. Six pitches.

And the First Annual Founders Day Semi-Professional Baseball Game was over. Clyde Mayberry had offered his gesture of partisanship, but he knew he could not accept the accusation of being a fool.

For the Tigers, the game ended quietly. They sat, or stood, and watched Happy Colquitt aim his Speed Graphic at Elmo, recording the final dejection of a man who had tried mightily and had failed. Elmo sat motionless, staring down, the portrait of Everyman whose work, at last, had crushed him, leaving him with a ruined arm and a broken spirit. He did not move until Ralph Claybank pushed his way through the crowd gathering around the Tigers' bench.

"It was a fine contest, Elmo," Ralph said. "Fine. Raybert says you need to go shake hands like gentlemen."

Elmo looked up at Ralph. He nodded and pulled himself up from the bench and motioned with his head and the Tigers followed him across the field toward the Bluejays' bench. He no longer cared that they were black. They were baseball players. Skin color had nothing to do with anything.

Runt Ashford did not have the same opinion. To Runt, black was black, white was white. He had made a drunken vow of vengeance if the Tigers lost and it was he who broke the after-game calm with a sudden bellow and a charge from behind the hogwire fence backstop, followed by a small mob of men eager for a fight.

Elmo whirled and saw Runt sprinting toward Monroe, waving a bicycle chain above his head, and he stepped in front of Monroe.

"What the hell you doing, Runt?" Elmo snarled. He dodged the swinging bicycle chain and hit Runt across the mouth with his left fist, feeling flesh split against the blow.

A thin, screaming man leapfrogged Runt's collapsing body and landed into Elmo. Elmo tried to break free, but another man caved into him. He could hear shouts of "Nigger lover, nigger lover..." A fist buried into his aching right arm. And then he felt bodies being ripped from him. He twisted to see Darby Robinson drop the thin, wiggling man like an insect. He could hear Otha's voice bellowing for the fight to stop and Happy shouting for the people in the bleachers to remain seated and above all other sounds, he could hear

Ralph's scream of panic. He had a mind-picture of Ralph running frantically in circles like a cartoon character in a picture show and for some inexplicable reason, he laughed.

"You all right?" Darby asked, effortlessly lifting Elmo from the ground.

"Yeah," Elmo said. He glanced toward Otha and saw Otha jerk his thirty-eight revolver from its holster and aim it in the air and pull the trigger. The shot exploded and echoed and the fighting stopped abruptly.

Elmo made a sweeping look across the infield. He saw the Tigers—his team—completely surround the Bluejays, corralling them in a tight circle. Washington Doubletree stood behind Sonny Jim Wallace, towering over him, and in the way memory plays unexpected tricks, Elmo thought of a childhood story his mother had told him about a gnat protecting an eagle, and he knew what he was seeing was an image he would keep forever, replaying it when there would be a need to think of a proud moment in his life.

He twisted back to Otha. Otha held his revolver over his head, pointed skyward. A blackjack was in his left hand. There were two bodies at his feet, writhing in the dirt. The look on Otha's face was the look of a dare, the same look of a cowboy sheriff who had just cleaned out a saloon in a cowboy motion picture show. If anybody else wanted to take up the argument, Otha was ready.

"Now, boys," Otha began in a stern, even voice, "this little scrap's over. Right now. Next man that even looks like he's gonna cause trouble has got six months on the road gang and I'll personally guarantee it, and I don't give a hoot in hell what color he is." He paused and scanned the crowd, letting his gaze stop on Runt. "Do I make myself clear?" he added.

"What's the matter with you?" Runt hissed. "Them's a bunch of niggers."

"Runt, I'm warning you," Otha growled.

"You better watch your back," Runt snarled. "They ain't but one of you."

Otha leveled his arm and placed the barrel of his revolver against Runt's temple. "You wrong, Runt. There's me and there's this." He cocked the hammer on his pistol. "You better learn how to count."

Runt's face paled. He stumbled backward. He turned to Moody Hickman. "You boys gonna take this?" he raged. "You just gonna take this without doing nothing?"

Moody stepped close to Runt. "Listen, you miserable little cockroach," he growled in a low, mean voice, "we got beat by the best damned baseball team you ever set eyes on. That's all."

"I told you, it's over, Runt," Otha said. "Another word—just one—and you're gonna be in cuffs."

Runt rolled his shoulders and bobbed his head. He glared at Otha, then turned defiantly and pushed his way through the crowd. A number of men followed him.

"There goes trouble," Elmo said to Otha.

"Could be," agreed Otha, "but he'll likely settle for bragging. All a man like Runt wants is to be as big as his words, but he's done stopped growing." He crossed the infield to Monroe. "Sorry this happened," he said. "You give us a good game, like we wanted."

"Nothing's hurt," Monroe said slowly. He made a half-circle in small, weary steps, surveying his team, still surrounded by the Tigers. "Me and the boys, we'll be going on now," he added.

"Not yet," Elmo told him.

Monroe frowned. The frown was a question.

"We got a barbecue to go to," Elmo said.

No one spoke. No one moved.

"You like barbecue, Monroe?" asked Elmo.

"I do, for sure," Monroe said, smiling.

"Mr. Claybank's buying," Elmo said.

Monroe shifted his weight, right leg to left leg, and there was pain in the movement. He raised his head and looked off in the distance, beyond the crowd. He could see a ribbon of smoke, like a scratch against the blue of the sky, wiggling up from Emmett Mulherne's barbecue stand. He nodded once, then turned back to Elmo. "Wonder what they'd say about all this up in Cuttercane?" he said softly.

"Not much telling," Elmo replied.

"It'll be something," Monroe said. He wagged his head. "Yessir. It'll be something."

Elmo chuckled. He leaned over and picked up Monroe's three-legged milking stool and handed it to him. "You right about that," he said. "You sure are."

Princess Salome Changes Her Act

The Story of
Mattie Mae Blair

Flema De Forrester believed she had been a nun in her former life, and being isolated in an Italian convent was likely the reason she had chosen her profession as an exotic dancer in the contemporary world.

"It's a well-known scientific social theory that people change one hundred and eighty degrees in different lives," Flema pontificated. "Saint in one, sinner in the other. Rich in one, poor in the other. White in one, black in the other. That's the way it goes. Ping-ponging around. Whatever you are right now, you can bet your sweet derriere you were just the opposite the last time around."

The name on Flema's Arkansas birth certificate was Flema Muriel Forrest, but she had made cosmetic changes to both name and body in the dozen years of playing club dates from San Francisco to New Jersey. Her stage name was Maiden Taiwan, given to her by a club owner in New Orleans. It took Flema a month to understand the humor.

To her male-dominated audiences, her name did not matter. They wanted only to see her undressing, from skintight gowns to G-strong and pasties. Flema had the body for it. She was a flesh-and-silicone marvel, astonishingly proportioned at 41-23-36, over five feet, nine inches in spike heels. Men yodeled like Tarzan at the sight of Flema. Women gasped in awe.

The silicone embedded in Flema's abundant breasts had restricted her command of twirling tassels and she had graduated to the more captivating art of belly twitching. It had transformed her from supporting act to star. Flema was a contortionist who could do more with her abdomen than a hungry python and when she performed her agonizing but inviting backbend routine, her body screamed to every man in the room. Feet spread, hands waving in little spirals like fluttering bird wings, Flema would stand center stage and begin swaying in slow jazz time, sending her belly into small waves of convulsions. Then she would begin to lean backward, her shoulders pushing against the air as though an invisible lover was forcing her down. The grand finale occurred when Flema put her hands flat on an eighteen-inch platform behind her. She would be perfectly arched backward, like the top half of a capital O. Her siliconed 41s looked like two white footballs on kickoff tees.

Wendell James listened and watched as Flema dressed for the midnight show and talked of her former life as a nun. Wendell managed Club Uptown in Atlanta. He was tall and thin and wore an ill-fitting wig. He also had problems with great thoughts and when Flema became obsessed with matters of reincarnation—as she often did—bewilderment crawled over his face in red splotches.

"How does that work, Flema?" asked Wendell. "Are you a rich, black saint in one life and a poor, white sinner in another? Or is it vice-the-versa?"

"It can be anything," Flema answered impatiently. "Nobody knows, except the spirits."

"What about the Chinese, Flema? They not black and they not white."

Flema flashed a tube of lipstick and darted it across her full, protruding lips.

"Wendell, you don't know the first thing about the occult, do you?" she said. "The Chinese only have one life."

"That's crazy, Flema."

"No, it's not," Flema argued. "There's so many Chinese, if they were reincarnated time after time, they'd be worse than flies. You couldn't stir them with a ten-foot pole."

Wendell shook his head in disbelief. He said, "You know, Flema, if that was so, I would of heard about it somewhere along the way, or I would of read about it in the *National Enquirer.*"

Flema flipped her G-string like a rubber band and did a full, admiring turn in front of the mirror. "You are the dumbest man I've ever met," she said. "Hand me that sequined thing."

Wendell tossed the sequined robe to her and Flema slipped into it and began stroking her legs, straightening the net stockings. "You really think you lived in another time?" he asked seriously.

"Absolutely," she answered. "I know it. I was put under one time and I spoke Italian."

"Put under?" Wendell said.

"Hypnotized," Flema replied. "Wo Fung did it. We worked a club together in California."

"Never heard of him."

"Wo Fung? He's great. He can put anybody under. Came from Chinatown in Frisco. You ought to get him over here, Wendell."

"I'll think about it," Wendell mumbled. "Did he have any other lives?"

Flema paused and stared thoughtfully at a pastie she had in her hand. "I don't know," she said earnestly. "He's a Chinaman, so I doubt it, but he told me one time that he had some Indian blood in him. Apache, I think. Anyway, everyone who knows anything at all, knows the Indians have more lives than any race on Earth. Indians have always been around Wendell. They were here a long time before the white man showed up."

"I do believe I'm aware of that, Flema," Wendell said smugly. "So what happened when he put you under and you started talking Italian? What'd you say?"

"How should I know?" Flema snapped. "I was under. Anyway, Wo Fung said I'd floated so far back in the reaches of my memory that it might be disturbing to remember any of it. He didn't want me to be tormented." She turned to look at Wendell. "You do understand that, don't you?"

Wendell shrugged. He lit a cigarette and let the smoke seep from his lips. Then he said, "Wait a minute, Flema. How do you know it even happened if you don't remember anything about it? Maybe Wo Fung was just trying to get past your G-string."

"That's stupid," Flema snarled. She glared at Wendell. "I know because Wo Fung said he'd listened to every word."

Wendell cocked his head in disbelief. He said, "A Chinaman with Apache Indian blood speaking Italian?"

"He was Catholic," Flema answered triumphantly. "The Pope speaks Italian."

Wendell signed and clucked his tongue. "You are just plain crazy," he said. He crushed his cigarette into an ashtray. "And I got to put up with you for a month. I don't think I can take it."

Flema laughed sharply. "Tomorrow, you're going to be on your hands and knees thanking me for being here."

"Why?" Wendell asked suspiciously.

"You'll see," Flema said. "You'll see." She did a quick hip-bump toward Wendell and strolled out of the dressing room.

The following afternoon, Flema opened the door to Wendell's office. Her face was radiant. She was dressed in tight pants and a loose-fitting blouse.

"What do you want?" Wendell growled. "I'm busy."

"There's somebody I want you to meet," Flema told him.

"Who?"

"Somebody you're going to hire to work in my show. She just arrived."

"I'm not about to hire anybody, and you can bank on it," Wendell said flatly.

Flema smiled. She said, "What kind of night did you have last night?"

"It was all right," Wendell answered.

"All right? All right, my royal behind," Flema said. "This place was full. They were swinging from the rafters. I heard you tell somebody it was the best crowd you'd had since the last time I was here."

"So it was a good night. There was a convention in town," Wendell said irritably.

"Well, sweetheart, it's going to get a lot better," Flema cooed.

"I'm not hiring anybody, Flema," Wendell insisted.

Flema moved close to Wendell's desk. He could smell the thick odor of her perfume. Her eyes glittered between frames of blue mascara coating her eyelashes. "You will," she whispered, "or you won't have Maiden Taiwan to bring in the crowds."

"Flema, that's blackmail."

"Oh, shut up, Wendell," Flema hissed. "She won't cost you but three hundred a week and I will personally guarantee that out of my salary if she doesn't double it in drinks."

Wendell slouched wearily in his chair. He stared in resignation at Flema. "Where's she from?" he asked.

Flema smiled happily. "That's the beauty of it," she said. "She's from Georgia, a little town called Cuttercane, up near the Tennessee border. The newspaper will eat that up, Wendell. A little country girl turned exotic."

"I don't know," Wendell mumbled.

"Well, I do," Flema insisted. She leaned across the desk, letting her breasts dangle teasingly from her loose-fitting blouse. "Trust me," she whispered.

"What's her name?" asked Wendell.

"Mattie," Flema answered. "Mattie Mae Blair."

"That's her stage name?" Wendell said.

"No, silly, of course not. That's her real name and she insists on being called Mattie Mae. Has something to do with her grandmother on her mama's side. Her stage name is Princess Salome. I named her."

"The Baptists must love you," Wendell said dryly.

"The Baptists love Mattie Mae," Flema corrected.

"Let's go see her," Wendell said in resignation.

Flema had arranged for Mattie Mae Blair to be waiting in Flema's private dressing room, telling her, "Just be there, dressed sexy. That's all it'll take. I know Wendell."

And Flema was right.

Mattie Mae Blair was stunning. She was not sexy. Flema was sexy. Mattie Mae Blair was sensuous and Wendell knew the difference. He was a professional when it came to sexy versus sensuous. A sexy woman was someone who posed, who put a man's will to test and made him yearn to do something about it immediately. A sensuous woman did not have to pose. A sensuous woman *was*. Simply that: she *was*. And Mattie Mae Blair from Cuttercane, Georgia, *was*. The aura of sensuality radiated from her. It was in her perfume and in her breathing. It was in the swollen arch of her top lip, in the symmetrical perfection of hazel eyes fixed like hazy paintings in the gallery of her face. She had one flaw in her Sophia Loren features—a tantalizing ink-dot of a mole off the right turn of her chin. It begged to be touched.

"I've worked with a lot of dancers, Wendell, but this one could be the very best," Flema said proudly. "I found her in one of those sleazy joints down in New Orleans. Some drunk Italian, or Frenchman, or whatever he was, was threatening to pull her off the stage because he was claiming she belonged to him, and you know me, Wendell; I can't stand a man like that, thinking he's God's gift to women, thinking he can just snap his fingers and any woman in hearing distance will swoon at his feet. I literally drug her out of the place. I mean it. Out the backdoor." She paused and looked admiringly at Mattie Mae. "Have you ever see anything like her—other than me, I mean?" she added.

Mattie Mae was dressed in bikini panties and a see-through net robe. She was tall and moved with ballet grace. Her breasts were living creatures quivering with the rhythmic stroking of her heart. Her nipples were olive fountains. The drop from her breasts to the shave-line of her G-string had the awesome splendor of a surfer's wave off Wakiki. Her legs made Wendell tremble. Her legs were perfectly muscled.

Wendell had seen hundreds of naked women in Club Uptown and had seldom been impressed. To Wendell, a stripper—even those who insisted on being called exotic dancers—was a commodity in business, no different than a handkerchief or a hotdog. He had always believed in keeping his business and personal life separate and in fifteen years as owner-manager of Club Uptown, he had never taken a stripper to bed. Wendell's preference had been the hookers who frequented his club and even that had been, in part, business—a professional courtesy for reserved bar stools.

But Wendell had never seen Mattie Mae Blair and he could feel the blush of awe rising in his face.

"Quit staring and say hello, Wendell," Flema commanded.

Wendell did not speak. Mattie Mae Blair had moved too close to him and he had been caught in the vapor of her sensuality.

"Wendell, say hello," Flema said again.

"Uh, hello," Wendell stammered.

Mattie Mae gazed at Wendell. Her hazel eyes twinkled through her aura. She looked like Brenda Starr in the moon-night presence of her eye-patch, black-orchid lover. She opened her mouth and the moist, pink muscle of her tongue nudged out the word: "Hello."

"Uh, hello," Wendell said again.

"You said that," Mattie Mae whispered. "Please. Sit down." The pupils of her eyes shuttered slowly. "I'm so glad to meet you. Flema's told me so much about you."

Marlene Dietrich could not have been more inviting, more persuasive, more commanding in making the word *please* sound multi-syllabic and mysterious.

Wendell smiled foolishly. His face colored a light crimson.

"Wendell, sit down," Flema said.

Mattie Mae took Wendell's hand and coaxed him to a canvas chair with a faded star imprinted on the back band. Her touch was hot. Wendell's hand throbbed. He could feel his blood corpuscles multiplying.

"Flema wanted me to come along with her and see if you might give me a chance at the club," Mattie Mae said in a purr. "I'd give anything just to have a chance."

Wendell did not reply. He stared dumbly into the eyes of Mattie Mae Blair.

"You know what she was in her other life, Wendell?" asked Flema. "A broomstick. I swear she had to be. A broomstick without the first bump of a boob."

Wendell did not take his eyes off Mattie Mae. He tried, but he could not move them.

"Now, what we'll do is work as a team," Flema said, pacing the dressing room. "You bring on all those no-talent go-go dancers you've got hanging around and then Mattie Mae will come on and I'll wrap it up."

Wendell nodded hypnotically.

"Well, get out of here and draw up a contract for Mattie Mae," Flema ordered. "That's three-fifty for the first week and if we build up the crowd, Mattie Mae goes up to five hundred and I go to eight-fifty. You got that, Wendell?"

"Huh?" Wendell said absently.

"Mattie Mae starts at four hundred and goes to five-fifty in a week. I jump to nine hundred next week."

"Uh—yeah," Wendell whispered. "Yeah. Sure."

Mattie Mae Blair's orchestrated triumph over Wendell was Phase One in Flema's careful plan to promote her protégé. Phase Two was Vinnie Coltrane, the entertainment editor for *The Atlanta Chronicle*. In her previous appearances at Club Uptown, Flema had waged a relentless campaign to earn Vinnie's favor. She had sent wine to his table when he visited the club. She had written him tender notes of appreciation for running pictures of her in costume, though the photographs had been airbrushed by the art department to cover exposed flesh. She had even named a dance in Vinnie's honor—the Vinnie Nudge, a seductive push against an imaginary dance partner, using her thighs as pliers.

Flema's approach to Vinnie in her promotion of Mattie Mae was direct. On the following Monday morning, Flema and Mattie Mae dressed in their most revealing public clothing, a twin effect of matching gold lame pantsuits with thin halter straps supporting body-tight blouses cut in a V to their rib cages. Each had an imitation fox fur curled around her neck. Each wore gold-dyed high heel shoes with tapped spikes that clicked like castanets when they walked. And each had a baby bulldog leashed to a gold strap dotted with glass facsimiles of jewelry. At ten o'clock they marched into the newsroom of *The Atlanta Chronicle* with the air of society women supporting a worthwhile charity.

Their appearance stunned the newsroom into absolute silence. Fingers froze above the keys of typewriters. Conversations ended mid-sentence. Telephones were lowered from ears to laps. Eighty-seven people sucked in a startled breath in unison.

And at his desk near the rear of the newsroom, the eighty-eighth person—Vinnie Coltrane—looked up from an essay he was writing on the life of David Wark Griffith. He muttered, "Oh, Lord."

One hundred and seventy-four eyes from eighty-seven people followed Flema rushing toward Vinnie, with Mattie Mae following. Eighty-seven mouths exhaled a quiet sigh and Flema's shrill, glad voice rang like a bell and echoed off the walls: "Vinnie, you darling!"

Vinnie's face flushed. He glanced toward the glass wall of the managing editor's office. He could see Raymond Barnes's startled face, his nose pressed against the glass pane, making a circle of fog.

"Oh, Lord," Vinnie said again. He pulled close to his typewriter in a feeble gesture of defense.

"Vinnie, Vinnie, Vinnie," Flema cooed. "Stand up and give me a hug."

Vinnie stood reluctantly. He could feel the one hundred and seventy-four eyes on him, burning into him. He extended his hand to Flema, stiff-armed. Flema smiled sweetly, took his hand and pulled him forward over his typewriter. She then leaned to him and kissed him with full lips and tongue. Vinnie could taste the paint of her lipstick and the toothpaste of her tongue. His face flamed with embarrassment.

The telephone rang at Vinnie's desk. He smiled foolishly at Flema. "Excuse me," he said. He lifted the receiver. "Uh—hello," he stammered.

"Coltrane, you sonofabitch," the voice whispered. Vinnie recognized it as Benny Whitlow, the political editor.

"Uh—thank you," Vinnie said. "I—I'll get it for you in a few minutes." He replaced the receiver in its cradle, looked again at the managing editor's office. Raymond Barnes's face had disappeared behind the circle of fog. His eyes darted to Macy Darrows, the religion editor. Macy was glaring at him in horror.

"Ah—what a surprise," Vinnie said weakly.

"You don't know the half of it, honey," Flema replied seriously, lowering her voice. "I've got a story for you and I wanted to bring it down here personally, before anybody else got word of it and beat you to it."

"Flema, nobody else in this city writes about nightclubs but me," Vinnie said.

"Well, they will after they hear about this," Flema declared. Then: "Vinnie, I want you to meet a fellow Georgian, Mattie Mae Blair. Get us some chairs, honey. We've got a story you're going to love."

The interview with Mattie Mae and Flema lasted forty minutes, interrupted constantly by abusive telephone calls from across the newsroom, but, for Vinnie, it was an interview worthy of the effort to get it. He learned that Mattie Mae was from Cuttercane, that her father had left home when she was still a child and that her mother had struggled to rear her and her younger brother. She had graduated from high school with decent grades, but there had not been any money for college and she had taken work as a secretary to provide for her ailing mother and her younger brother, who had ambitions to be a racecar driver.

At work, Mattie Mae had discovered the power of her physical allure: men could not leave her alone. She had followed one to New Orleans, but was soon abandoned and forced to drift from menial job to menial job, from man to man, until, finally, she had entered an amateur contest for exotic dancers and had been such an instant hit that she was offered a job. For two years she had danced under the pseudonym of Honeycomb, lying to her mother about her work and about the man she was living with, a European with a hairy body and an annoying French-Dutch accent. "Her mother thought she was modeling clothes for a department store," Flema explained.

Then, one night, a man from Cuttercane wandered into the club and recognized her and Mattie Mae Blair's double life came to an end.

"She had to admit what was going on or give up the business," said Flema. "She chose to work."

"Well, that's interesting," Vinne said sympathetically.

"That's nothing, Vinnie," Flema enthused. "Guess how she got her body?"

Vinnie blushed.

"Not like me," Flema added quickly. "There's not an ounce of silicone there. Not one. But she used to weigh one hundred and eighty pounds when she was in high school."

Vinnie's eyebrows arched in surprise.

"That's right," Mattie Mae said softly. "I did. I was fat."

"Tell him what you did, honey," urged Flema.

Mattie Mae looked away. She stared into the eyes of Bill Curtis, sitting at a nearby desk. Bill snapped a pencil he was holding. Mattie Mae looked back at Vinnie.

"I went wading in Asa's Spring," she said calmly.

"In what?" asked Vinnie.

"Asa's Spring. It's a place just out of Cuttercane. People who live in that area believe it's got some kind of magical powers. If you want something bad enough and you wade in Asa's Spring, you'll get it. I wanted to lose weight, more than I'd ever wanted anything."

"And that was it?" Vinnie said.

Mattie Mae nodded.

"It just rolled off her," Flema added. "She came out of that water looking like she does now."

Mattie Mae smiled sweetly. "Not really, Flema," she corrected. "It took some time, but, yes, it happened."

"You really believe it was the water?" asked Vinnie.

Mattie Mae's eyes burned into him. She whispered, "I believe what I see in the mirror."

Flema's laugh spilled throughout the newsroom.

The call that ended the interview was from Raymond Barnes, ordering Vinnie to his office. Vinnie explained it as an emergency to Flema and Mattie Mae—a conference with the chief writers and editors of the paper, a major breaking story they wanted his advice on. He promised to attend their performance that evening, and then he ushered them through the newsroom to the elevator before rushing back to Raymond Barnes's office.

"Yes sir?" Vinnie said hesitantly.

"Coltrane," Raymond began in a stern voice, "just what the hell was that? I thought we were going to have tits dribbling across the floor like basketballs. Damned if I'll ever figure out what goes on out there with you."

"Sir?"

"You've had every freak in the South parade through this newsroom at one time or another, but damned if you didn't break the mold and flush it down the commode this time."

"I—I didn't know they were coming," Vinnie said defensively.

"Every man and boy out there is worthless as weak-old bread right now," Raymond snapped. "Carl Barber had to get a copyboy to bring him a glass of ice water. We can't have that kind of disruption. We've got a newspaper to put out."

"Yes sir," Vinnie said. An image of Carl Barber gulping ice water to cool his excitement flew into his mind. He smiled slightly.

"It's not a laughing matter that I can see," Raymond grumbled. He leaned forward over his desk. "Those dogs they had. They piss on the new carpet?"

Vinnie swallowed hard. The dogs had indeed pissed on the new carpet. The dogs had chewed holes in his socks and licked at the polish on his shoes. "I, ah, don't know," he whined. "Maybe. A little."

171

"Then get a fistful of paper towels and get it up, boy," Raymond ordered. "If I have to bring in a carpet cleaner, it's coming out of your salary."

The story that Vinnie wrote—from Mattie Mae's telling and Flema's embellishment—was a sad song of a country girl forced into slavery of the flesh. It was a story of circumstances, of shattered dreams and ambitions, of determination and ultimate triumph, and it was clean enough for Mattie Mae to send to her mother with pride. He balanced the aura of Mattie Mae's sensuality with a commentary on virtues of basic, middle-America values and then he closed with a couple of paragraphs about Mattie Mae's dignity being greater than her environment. To enhance the hometown sentiment angle, he called Frank Marsh, the chief of police of Cuttercane, and asked how the citizens of Cuttercane felt about Mattie Mae.

"They's them that's against her and they's them that's for her," Frank told him. "But speaking for myself and most of the boys around here, she's something. Yes sir, she is. She's something else."

Even the photograph of Mattie Mae that Vinnie chose to accompany the story had character. It was a closeup of her face, emphasized with soft lighting to make it look like the subject of a lonely blues tune.

Vinnie's story was one of imagination and fiction, hinged on truth. Yet it was a story with an internal voice, like a lyrical poem that swims into the eyes and then into the brain and then into the soul. And it was a story that lured people into the crowded, smoky lounge of Club Uptown off Luckie Street in the epicenter of Atlanta, Georgia. Mattie Mae Blair, in the persona of Princess Salome, was someone who had to be seen.

Mattie Mae expressed her appreciation to Vinnie by sending him a personal hand-printed note containing the words, *Your a Doll,* and a bottle of Canadian Club blended whiskey, most likely swiped from Club Uptown's stock room.

Flema was not as pleased as Mattie Mae. She called Vinnie and screamed, "You sonofabitch, you've never done anything like that for me."

Vinnie tried to explain that Flema was not from Georgia and had not been forced into exotic dancing, which had been the thesis of his story on Mattie Mae.

"If you remember, it was you who came up with that angle," Vinnie suggested gently.

"I don't give a damn," complained Flema. "I thought you were my friend. You must have been a eunuch in some other form of life, and you can kiss my prissy tail."

A flutter of anger roiled in Vinnie. He replied icily, "I will, if it's not in surgery."

Flema's distress was great. She felt betrayed and she knew that her status as Club Uptown's feature attraction was eroding with the ascending stardom of Princess Salome. She broke her contract with Wendell and left for Miami, vowing never to return to Atlanta.

"She's crazy," Wendell grumbled to Vinnie. "Kept saying that I was about to reduce her to second-billing."

"Were you?" asked Vinnie.

"In time," Wendell confessed.

With Flema's leaving, Mattie Mae became the headline act at Club Uptown and her popularity was like an uncontrollable brush fire. She was beautiful and gifted and her sensuality spilled from the stage in lapping waves of perfumed heat. Drunks proposed to her from their tables. College boys begged for a pasty to hang from their belts like some fraternity ribbon . Civilized married men made paper airplanes of crisp, new dollar bills and sailed them at her and vowed they were going home at the end of the evening and throw bricks at their wives. Conventioneers appeared in tour buses and left to tell other conventioneers of Princess Salome's veil dance. Club Uptown was crowded from happy hour until closing. Wendell was ebullient.

Mattie Mae Blair—Princess Salome—was a star and she believed that Vinnie Coltrane was responsible.

"Every man I meet wants to take me to bed," she lamented. "Everybody but you, Vinnie. You're the only man I can trust."

"I wouldn't think of me as being that noble," Vinnie warned. "I mean, I am a man, too. It's just that, well, you know, it'd be a conflict of interest."

"Oh," Mattie Mae replied.

"Never mix business with pleasure, Mattie Mae," Vinnie told her. "That's my creed."

"We'll just be friends, then," Mattie Mae replied. "I just want you to be there when I need you, the way real friends are."

"I will. Don't worry," Vinnie assured her. "You try me. You'll see."

A month later, Vinnie received a telephone call from Wendell.

"Vinnie, you got to get to the club," Wendell begged.

"What for?" asked Vinnie. "It's eleven o'clock at night. I've got a movie review to finish for tomorrow."

"It's Mattie Mae," Wendell told him. "She's been asking for you."

"What's wrong?"

"Wrong? She's drunk," Wendell bellowed. "She's been drinking wine all day and she's sloshed. She's supposed to go on in an hour."

"Put somebody on in her place," Vinnie advised. "Say she's sick."

"Are you kidding me?" Wendell snapped. "I've got a reunion of some old soldier boys that survived Iwo Jima and a couple of other landings. They've come from all over the country to see her. She don't show up, they'll tear the place apart. There's already been a couple of fights."

"Why me, Wendell?" Vinnie asked in exasperation.

"Because you're the one she wants," Wendell said. He paused and Vinnie could hear him sucking his lips. "Damn it," he moaned. "Why do I have to have all the luck?"

"All right," Vinnie agreed. "For a few minutes."

"I'll buy you a steak," Wendell told him.

"No, Wendell, I can't do that. Conflict of interest."

"And a bottle of wine."

"No, Wendell."

"We'll talk about it later," Wendell said. "Get here."

Mattie Mae was exactly as Wendell had described her: drunk. Weaving drunk. Glazed-eyed drunk. Mumbling drunk. She was beating on the door of Wendell's office when Vinnie arrived.

"I had to lock her in," Wendell said. "She was wandering around, bawling, telling everybody they ought to be ashamed for being here."

"That's exactly how I feel, Wendell," Vinnie said.

Wendell shrugged. He opened the door to his office and stepped behind Vinnie.

"Vinnie," Mattie Mae said in a sob. She threw her arms around his neck. "Vinnie, Vinnie, Vinnie." She smelled like sour wine. Her great breasts heaved against Vinnie's chest.

"All right," Vinnie said. He folded his arms awkwardly around her. "I'm here. What's wrong?"

Mattie Mae's sobbing increased. Her voice was a moan—"I'm so sorry, Vinnie. So sorry, so ashamed."

"Don't be," Vinnie told her. "Come on, sit down, talk to me." He offered a light, put-on laugh. "You know you're making Wendell jealous, don't you?"

Mattie Mae nuzzled her face deeper into Vinnie's shoulder. "Do you hate me, Vinnie?" she asked

"Of course not," Vinnie said.

Wendell rolled his desk chair behind her. "Damn it, Mattie Mae, sit down," he ordered. "You're dripping mascara all over the place."

"It'd just kill me if you hated me," Mattie Mae whimpered.

"Well, I don't, so forget that," said Vinnie. "You're one of my favorite people, and I mean that."

"Would you hold me?" Mattie Mae begged. "Close. Really close." She pulled Vinnie tight against her, rolled her face into his chest, leaving streaks of makeup on his shirt.

"Good Lord, Mattie Mae, are you crazy?" hissed Wendell. "This is the newspaper. You're gonna blow any chance I ever had of getting a little publicity." He turned to Vinnie. "Hey, I'm sorry. I'll take care of her, if you want to leave."

"It's all right," Vinnie said. "It's the wine talking. I'm not paying any attention. Look, get me some cold wet towels and strong coffee and leave me alone with her for a few minutes."

"I don't know," Wendell said warily.

"Wendell, just do what I asked," Vinnie countered. "She'll be all right."

It took twenty minutes of coaxing and soft pleading for Vinnie to get cold compresses wrapped around Mattie Mae's elbows and knees and to calm her. She curled her legs under her in Wendell's chair and sat very still. Her face was flushed with wine, but she was still beautiful.

"What's the matter?" Vinnie asked quietly. "Why'd you do this?"

Mattie Mae was quiet for a moment. She stared vacantly across the room. Then she began to speak in a whisper. "It's—it's my life," she said. "I'm—no good. No good at all, Vinnie. I'm cursed, like Mama said I was."

"Cursed?" Vinnie asked. "How?"

"By some kind of evil demon," Mattie Mae answered. "Mama keeps telling me it'll catch up with me, what I'm doing."

"Well, that's just a mama being worried about her child," Vinnie offered.

A deep, sudden sob erupted from Mattie Mae. She said, "Mama thinks I'm—"

Vinnie took her hand and began to stroke it with his fingers.

"She thinks I'm a whore," Mattie Mae added painfully. Another sob erupted from her, more painful than the first. "I'm not that way, Vinnie. I'm not. I like men, but I'm not that way."

"Of course not," Vinnie replied. "Don't think about it. You're a beautiful woman. It's not your fault that men pay attention to you."

There was a pause, a long silent moment.

"Anything else?" Vinnie asked quietly.

Mattie Mae touched her face with her fingertips. She looked up to Vinnie. "Do you know about him?"

"About who?" asked Vinnie.

"Him. The man in New Orleans. He was my lover for a long time."

"That's all right," Vinnie said. "You don't need to think about things like that."

"He owns a bicycle shop," Mattie Mae whispered in a forlorn voice.

A pulse of anger slapped at Vinnie, and the feeling surprised him. He was fond of Mattie Mae, but had never been jealous of the men who fawned over her.

"I still hear from him," Mattie Mae added. "He calls me every week or so. He wants me to come live with him."

"Is that what you want?" asked Vinnie.

For a moment, Mattie Mae did not speak. She turned her face away from Vinnie. Her eyes coated with moisture. "I—I don't know," she said quietly. "Sometimes, that's what I want. Sometimes, I want something else. Sometimes I want to be away from all of it."

"Don't think about it," Vinnie advised.

"It's like I got two people living inside me," she said. "And I want to be both of them."

"That'd be hard to do," Vinnie offered. An image of Mattie Mae making love to a dark, broad-faced man billowed in his mind. An involuntary twitch rippled across his chest.

Mattie Mae removed one of the cold washcloths from her elbow and dotted it across her forehead. After a moment, she said, "Do you like my act, Vinnie? I mean, really?"

"It's fine," Vinnie assured her. "Really. I mean it."

"I'm tired of it," Mattie Mae said suddenly. "I want to do something different."

"Well, then, you should," Vinnie said, forcing his voice to be easy and casual. He was glad to be talking of something other than the man in New Orleans. "Maybe the same old routine does get a little boring," he added.

"What can I do?" Mattie Mae asked thoughtfully.

Vinnie moved behind her and began to massage her shoulders. The image of the dark, broad-faced man slipped by his face and disappeared from the room. He said, "What can you do? Let's see. You could do something that's completely different."

"Oh, I like that," Mattie Mae enthused. "Like what?"

Vinnie paused in his massage. "Well," he said in a light voice, "you could go out nude and then put your clothes on. Just reverse the act."

Mattie Mae laughed easily. She reached up to touch his hand resting on her shoulder. "You're funny."

Vinnie resumed his massaging. "You could rub a little baby oil on you. When the lights hit you, you'd be glowing. That'd make them sit up and take notice."

Mattie Mae snickered, then she laughed aloud, a little girl's laugh. She turned to Vinnie. "You're sweet," she said. "You really are. Taking all this time to help me."

"Glad to do it," Vinnie said. "You all right now?"

"I'm fine," Mattie Mae told him. "Really. I'll have one little sip of wine to steady my nerves and I'll be ready for the show."

Vinnie frowned. "I don't think the wine is a good idea."

Mattie Mae smiled and pulled Vinnie to her and kissed him on the cheek. "Believe it or not," she said, "it's the way I sober up. Will you stay for the show?"

"It's kind of late," Vinnie replied. "I've still got a story to do."

"Just for the show, Vinnie. Please. I want you to."

"I guess," Vinnie said hesitantly. Then: "Yeah, sure."

"Vinnie?"

"Yeah?"

"I'm glad you're my friend. Before I leave Atlanta, I want us to go to some nice place for dinner."

Vinnie smiled. A blush shot across his face. He thought: *It would have been nice dating her under other circumstances. She would have been easy to fall in love with.*

"I hope that doesn't make you feel uncomfortable," Mattie Mae said, "and I know I shouldn't be saying such things, but I like you. I have from the first time we met."

"I like you, too, Mattie Mae," Vinnie told her.

Wendell was astonished to see Mattie Mae walk proudly from his office to her dressing room. He moved a table to stage-side for Vinnie and ordered a glass of wine and a steak.

"Anything he wants, he gets," Wendell told the waitress. "And wrap up a bottle of Canadian Club for him to take when he leaves."

"Wendell, I can't accept that," Vinnie protested. "It's a conflict of interest. In fact, it's bribery."

"Forget the Canadian Club," Wendell yelled after the waitress. He sat at the table with Vinnie. "What'd you do?" he asked. "I can't believe she's sober."

"Nothing," Vinnie told him. "Talked to her. That's all."

"What about them cold bath cloths?"

"Wrapped them around her elbows and knees," Vinnie explained. "It's good for nausea."

"You're kidding me," Wendell exclaimed. "I'll remember that. You think she'll be all right for the show?"

"You saw her," Vinnie said confidently. "Sure. She'll be fine. She said she'd have a sip of wine to calm her and then she'd be ready to go on."

Wendell bolted from his seat. "A sip of wine?" he cried hysterically. "My God, Vinnie, she's a wino. Don't you know that?"

"Settle down, Wendell. She promised to take just a sip," Vinnie said. "I don't mean to sound arrogant, but I trust her."

Wendell sucked on his lips. He stroked his bushy wig and sat down. "I hope you're right," he mumbled.

"Don't sweat it," Vinnie said.

A woman with the stage name of Love Lady opened the show. Known for twenty years on the club circuit as a has-been, Love Lady had lost control of her body, but yards of satin costuming disguised her spastic efforts at dance and she filled out her act with obscene gesturing. Her big number was to the accompaniment of *In the Mood*.

180

From the reaction of the audience, no one was. The reunion of old soldiers booed her off the stage.

"I got to fire her," Wendell mumbled. "Or put her in an old age home."

A pock-faced comedian named Mo Horton followed Love Lady. He tried to tell clever jokes about sex, but the crowd did not care to hear about sex; they wanted to see it. Wendell cut Mo's act by fifteen minutes with a signal to the band. Mo sneered at Wendell as he slithered off stage.

Lucy Fender, who worked under the pseudonym of Little Delight and had second-billing on the show, took center stage. The veterans of World War Two loved her. They whistled and screamed and threw popcorn at the stage. Since Flema had abdicated her feature role at Club Uptown and Mattie Mae had been elevated to be the star attraction, Lucy had become obsessed with competition. She had added a couple of acrobatic moves inspired by drawings from the Karma Sutra that defied laws of anatomy, and on this night, with the cheering of inebriated aging soldiers, she was unbelievable. She used the stage like an animal on prowl. She crawled, slithered, bumped, hunched, oohed, touched, begged, dared. It was a pornographic movie, with all the roles performed in Lucy's shimmering, living flesh, and just as she threatened madness, she abruptly stopped. She did a commanding turn and glared at the audience, a haughty queen surveying her subjects, and then she marched offstage.

Mo Horton, who was the club's emcee as well as its comedian, was as startled as everyone by Lucy's performance. "Ladies and gentlemen," he shouted over the roar, "I've worked with Little Delight for years and I'm telling you, she's never before been this great. Let's hear it for Little Delight. Come on! Bring her back."

Mo was parading the stage, shouting, whistling into the microphone, and the audience joined him. The applause was deafening in the room. Someone threw an old army hat on stage. "Little Delight, Little Delight!" they shouted.

Lucy stepped regally from the wings and did a couple of hip bumps that Weyman Fuller picked up on his drums and sent rolling in sync across the club. Lucy's face was damp with perspiration. She walked to the front railing of the stage and flicked her finger across her forehead and sent a spray of perspiration into the audience. It was an unnatural gesture for Lucy, but her subjects howled for more and Lucy stalked the apron of the stage, flicking perspiration. At one stage-side table, she knelt and took the head of a balding man and rubbed his face across her heaving breasts. The man looked as though he had had a coronary. Mo was yelling, "Little Delight, make my night, make my night!" and Weyman was pounding his bass drum savagely, keeping rhythm with every gesture Lucy made. Wendall sat watching in awe. He leaned to Vinnie and whispered, "She's good."

"She is," Vinne agreed.

It took five minutes to get Lucy offstage and to calm the audience from the racy high of her act. Then Mo stepped to center stage and Harry Swanson, the pianist, kicked the lighting controls under his left foot. The stage dimmed to a single spot on Mo.

"Ladies and gentlemen," Mo intoned from a cave in his chest, "I don't know of anyone can really follow that act, not even Bridget Bardot—anyone, that is, except the star of our show, and even she has a great challenge." He paused and beamed a smile toward stage left. "But the great artists always respond and I know tonight will be no different," he added.

Mo tossed his head dramatically. The spotlight glistened over his greased-down hair. He switched the microphone from his downstage hand to his upstage hand. He cleared his throat to deepen his voice. Harry began a casual vamp on the piano, muted by the soft petal. Mo said, "Ladies and gentlemen, it's time for Club Uptown to present one of the most tantalizingly beautiful women ever to grace a stage anywhere in the world—from Las Vegas, Nevada, to Miami, Florida, from the French Riveria to the seductive Bahamas. A woman of such breathtaking proportions that men have fainted in her presence and women have bowed in admiration. Princes have asked for her hand in marriage. Hollywood producers and directors send her offers every day of the week—"

"Where'd he get all of that?" Vinnie whispered to Wendell.

Wendell beamed. "I wrote it. Sounds good, don't it?"

"Ladies and gentlemen," Mo continued, turning back to the audience, his face a mask of excitement, "for your exclusive pleasure, Club Uptown proudly, happily, enthusiastically presents the one, the only, the most beautiful woman of them all—Princess Salome!"

"Lord, that's good stuff," Wendell cried joyfully.

Mo had worked the crowd like a used car salesman. Old soldiers, drunk with whiskey and memories, leaped to their feet, filling the room with yells and whistles. They pounded the tables with beer bottles, eager to throw themselves into the frenzy that Lucy had created and Mattie Mae was ready to continue.

Harry hit a switch with his left foot and the baby spots embracing the stage began to flutter off and on, dotting the stage with teasingly hot colors. Weyman dropped in a drumroll that had the sound of gathering thunder out of invisible lightning. Harry hammered the piano and the pure, screaming cry of Wolf Phillips' trumpet split the stale air of Club Uptown. It was music frozen in its intensity—hard, punishing, steaming. Harry quickly punched at another switch with his foot controls and the fluttering lights died away as a fingerspot winked open on the stage left curtain where Princess Salome would make her entrance.

Every eye in Club Uptown—from old soldiers and conventioneers, from college boys and married men making moves on hookers and from the hookers themselves, and from bartenders and waitresses—was fixed in a stare at the bubble of the fingerspot.

Suddenly, a net robe filled the white glare of the spot, billowed open and floated gently to the floor.

A great roar rose up in Club Uptown.

"More! More! More!"

A bra whipped through the funnel of light, then a G-string, followed by two shoes, two pasties, two net stockings and a shower of colorful veils. Harry and Weyman and Wolf where handcuffed to the downbeat.

"What's she doing?" Wendell said in a faltering voice. He was glued to his seat.

A slippery, oily leg sprang into sight from the curtain.

"Oh, my God," Vinnie whispered in horror. "Oh, my God."

The leg went rigid, then relaxed slowly, bending at the knee in a motion that seemed to draw Mattie Mae's body forward with it. Harry and Weyman and Wolf broke off the downbeat and vaulted into a raunchy bastardization of *Not as a Stranger*. On the fourth note, Mattie Mae did a pirouette out of the doorway and stopped full in the dead center of the fingerspot.

She was nude.

Completely nude.

Her body was coated with baby oil and she glistened like a goddess.

Her honey-blond hair rolled over her shoulders and she struck a pose like a Roman statue. Harry tried to kick out the light, but missed the control and stepped on the master switch. The stage exploded in brightness. No one had ever seen anyone as incredible as Princes Salome without her veils. Compared to Princess Salome, Marilyn Monroe looked like Little Orphan Annie.

There was a moment of stunned silence in the room, a concerted gasp, then turmoil. Voices exploded like bombs. Men fell from their chairs. Tables were overturned.

Wendell began to hyperventilate. His body was heaving. His wig fell off. Vinnie caught him and settled him back in his chair.

Mo rushed onstage, shouting "Stop the show! Stop the show! Against the law! Against the law!"

A former Private First Class crawled on top of his table and screamed, "Throw the bastard out." His companions took up the chant and began to beat on their tables with bottles and glasses. Mo became confused. He dropped his rage and turned to face the mob, smiling benevolently. He raised the microphone to his mouth and said in his deep emcee voice, "Fellows, we just can't allow this. It's against the law. Got to have pasties and g-strings."

An ashtray sailed through the air and Mo ducked and dashed for stage left. He grabbed at Mattie Mae's extended arm and yanked. His grasp slipped through the baby oil and he crashed into the curtain. He jumped up and lunged at Mattie Mae, trying to body-tackle her. Mattie Mae squirmed with a flawless hip-bump and Mo zipped past her and plunged into Weyman's drums.

"Let's get him, boys," the Private First Class bellowed.

Mattie Mae was dancing around the stage in a daze. She began calling, "Vinnie said I should do it. Vinnie said it would be all right." She peered into the audience. "Vinnie? Vinnie? Where are you?"

Vinnie slipped under his table, pulling the tablecloth around him.

"Get off the stage, Mattie," Harry hissed. "The cops are gonna close this place down, you idiot."

The Private First Class broad-jumped from his table to the stage, landing in front of Harry. "Shut your face!" he ordered.

Harry hit the Private First Class with a sheet of music and the former veteran of the Pacific theater roared at the insult. He grabbed Harry by his jacket and slung him across the stage.

Club Uptown was a war zone.

Once-upon-a-time soldiers, made young again by alcohol and memories, rose up in unison and began to storm the stage as though it was a Japanese stronghold under the command of Emperor Mo Horton.

Sprawled on the floor near the stage, still hyperventilating, Wendell saw the invasion and whispered, "Oh, my God." He crawled under the table with Vinnie.

A cry of assault filled the room.

And then the invasion abruptly stopped.

It stopped because Wolf had ducked behind the piano with his trumpet and, safe from flying bottles and glasses and ashtrays, he began to play *The Star-Spangled Banner* with a power that was almost spiritual in its intensity.

At the first three notes, the ex-soldiers froze in their rush to rescue Mattie Mae. They snapped to attention, threw salutes across their faces. A Shriner, who was with his own wife, stood at his table and removed his tasseled hat and placed it over his heart.

"Vinnie said I could do it," Mattie Mae said again in a pitifully weak voice. "He did." She held her goddess pose. "It's a new act," she added sweetly. The lights shimmered over her slippery body.

Someone whispered, "Shhhhhhhhhhhhhhh."

Wolf emerged from behind the piano, edging close to Mattie Mae. He was playing with energy that only fear could give a man. He hit notes Al Hirt had never heard. He trebled. He vamped. He soared in the sweet, searing skies of the jazzman on a high.

A silence fell over Club Uptown. The only sound was from the voice of Wolf's trumpet and his trumpet was overwhelming. It was exuberant, joyful, triumphant. Wolf was playing from his chest and from his guts and from his toes. He turned to look at Mattie Mae. A string of tears, like baby pearls, streamed from her eyes. She was standing perfectly erect, her right hand resting on her slippery left breast. And then she began to sing in a shrill but surprisingly good imitation of an operatic soprano: "Oooooooh, say can you see...."

The Shriner, also weeping, joined her, then the Shriner's wife and the Private First Class, then Harry and Weyman and Mo, and then everyone in Club Uptown.

"Whose broad stripes and bright stars ..."

And that was when the police arrived, storming through the door.

"...thro' the perilous fight..."

"What the hell's this?" demanded an angry sergeant.

A hooker standing at attention beside her bar stool hushed him with a raised hand. The sergeant glared at her, but stood quietly, fidgeting with his nightstick.

"...were so gallantly streaming..."

The sergeant removed his cap. He looked up at Mattie Mae and saw that she was nude. His mouth opened in shock. A guttural sound, like pain, crawled from his throat. The rest of the raiding police party stood awkwardly behind their sergeant, waiting, holding their caps over their hearts. One of them whispered, "God Almighty, look at that broad."

Wendell peeked from under the table as Mattie Mae led the crowd in:

"...lannnnd of the freeeeeeee and the hommmme of the brrraaave..."

"Vinnie, I'm a dead duck," whispered Wendell.

"You are unless they know another verse," Vinnie said, handing Wendell his wig.

After the raid on Club Uptown, Wendell sent a bottle of Canadian Club to Vinnie with a note that read: "For Vinnie, who got us in the news and gave us turn-away crowds. Why don't you drop back in?"

Vinnie felt both guilty and lucky. Because of the World War Two reunion crowd, no one had been arrested in the raid on Club Uptown and Wendell had taken responsibility for Mattie Mae's behavior. Still, the news of Vinnie's presence at the club had wiggled its way back to the newspaper and Raymond Barnes had delivered a stern lecture on morality and professional conduct.

"We've got to get you off that beat, Coltrane," Raymond had said, "or you won't be worth a damn by the time you're thirty."

"Beats politics and sports," Vinnie had replied, attempting humor.

"Don't get smart," Raymond had snapped. "I could put you on obits or religion."

In the weeks that followed, Mattie Mae and Lucy became the most popular show in the history of Atlanta nightclubs. "Hotter than *Gone with the Wind*," Wendell boasted to Vinnie. "I'm thinking about having reservations to *make* reservations. We keep this up, I may start franchising."

Wendell had a right to be enthusiastic. Mattie Mae and Lucy were a perfect complement. Lucy was the warm-up and Mattie Mae the finish. Between them, they made the centerfolds of smut magazines seem like the posing of debutants in silk gowns. They were exactly what Wendell advertised them to be—sensational.

Vinnie did return to Club Uptown regularly and Mattie Mae spent hours attempting to amend the embarrassment she had caused him. In the process she forced Vinnie into situations that were equally as ticklish as her nude appearance on stage. Once she invited Vinnie to a dinner that a group of strippers were hosting to celebrate Love Lady's overdue retirement. Vinnie did not know it, but Mattie Mae had arranged for him to be a judge in a contest to determine which stripper had the most perfect body. She called Vinnie to the stage, handed him a tape measure and instructed the candidates to parade before him. Vinnie later told Wendell that it was the most memorable night of his life. "I swear to you, Wendell, I've never even thought about some of the things those women promised me if I'd fudge an inch or two in the right direction."

"I thought something was going on, the way you kept blushing," Wendell said. "But I don't remember who it was you picked."

"Lady Luck," Vinnie replied. "She needed the compliment."

On the night before she left Club Uptown for an engagement in Dallas, Texas, Mattie Mae hugged Vinnie in a tight, wiggling embrace and wept with gladness over the wonder of their friendship. "Please don't forget me," she begged. "I don't think I could bear it if you forgot me."

"And I don't think that's possible," Vinnie told her.

For a few weeks, Vinnie received letters from her, letters written in a friendly, simple manner, each marked with misspellings and poor grammar. In one of them, she reported that she had renewed her friendship with Flema in Dallas.

And then the letters stopped arriving.

One afternoon in early summer, Wendell appeared in the newsroom. He looked sad and tired and old.

"What's wrong?" asked Vinnie.

"Flema called," Wendell told him. "There's some bad news about Mattie Mae."

"What?"

"She was cut up in some bar down in New Orleans. Some fool went crazy. Really messed up her face."

"My God," Vinnie exclaimed. "How is she?"

"She'll live, but she won't never dance again," Wendell answered. "Can't cover up the scars." He shook his head. "What a waste," he sighed. "That was one beautiful woman. She should have been married to somebody rich enough to take care of her."

"I think you're right," Vinnie said softly.

In autumn, Vinnie learned from Wendell that Mattie Mae was living with her mother in Cuttercane and he persuaded Raymond Barnes that it would make a good feature story to do a follow-up on the tragedy of a lovely woman caught up in the meanness of nightclub life. "Maybe," Raymond agreed, "but for God's sake, tell the truth, Coltrane, or you'll be working a paper route in south Georgia when I get through with you."

In Cuttercane, Vinnie found Frank Marsh.

"Yeah, I remember talking to you," Frank said in the police station. "Got the story you wrote with my name in it over there in my desk drawer. Too bad about Mattie Mae. I seen her a couple of days ago. Still got the body, but there's a scar on her face that'd make a man throw a croker sack over her. I hear tell she was cut up on the arm, too, but she wears them long-sleeve blouses and you can't see it. Can't hide the face, though."

"Could you tell me where they live?" asked Vinnie. "I thought I'd go see her."

"Might be good for her," Frank admitted. He drew the directions for Vinnie on the back of a traffic ticket.

Mattie Mae was not at home. Her mother said she had gone to Asa's Spring. "Always going down there," she told Vinnie. "Got it in her head she'll get all right if she splashes around in that old waterhole. You want to see her, just drive on down the road about a mile. You'll see a sign saying where it is on your right. Follow that little woods road. You'll find it."

"I'll do that," Vinnie said.

The sign marking the turnoff to Asa's Spring was easy to spot, and Vinnie drove slowly down the narrow, grass-covered woods road that was lined by oak and poplar trees. He parked near a dust-covered Ford and got out of his car and walked along a thick stand of river cane until he stood on a slight knoll above the spring. He saw Mattie Mae sitting in the grass beside the spring, gazing into the water at the scarred reflection of her scarred face. He watched as she reached into the reflection and cupped water and lifted it to her face and rubbed her fingers over the scar.

Vinnie moved quietly toward her. "Mattie Mae," he said softly.

She turned in a jerk at the sound of his voice. He could see the livid slash across her left cheek. She quickly covered her face with her hand and ducked away from him.

"Leave me alone," she said.

Vinnie stepped closer to her. "I came to see you," he said.

"Don't look at me," she said in a stern, warning voice.

"I've already seen you. If I leave now, all I'll remember is your back turned to me."

"Go on, Vinnie. Leave me alone. I want to be by myself."

"Is it doing any good? Washing yourself like that?" Vinnie asked.

Mattie Mae did not answer. She stared at the glittering surface of the water.

"Is it?" Vinnie said.

"It might be. If I want it bad enough, it will," she whispered.

"Was it true, what you told me before?" Vinnie asked. "About losing weight, I mean?"

Mattie Mae nodded slowly. "It happened then. Maybe it will again."

"It's not the same thing, Mattie Mae. Maybe you were just at the age to start changing. This is different. That's nothing but water."

"No, it's not," Mattie Mae said quickly. "It's not."

"Is it good to drink?" he asked.

"It's all right," she told him. She paused. "It's cold."

191

Vinnie moved to the spring, but he did not look at Mattie Mae. He kneeled and cupped water in his hand and sipped from it. It was cold, as Mattie Mae had said, and sweet as fruit water is sweet; he could feel it burning at the back of his eyes. "Good," he said. "It's good." He turned to Mattie Mae. "Look at me," he whispered.

She lifted her face to him. The scar across her cheek did not seem as deep or as hideous as he thought. It was merely a thin, curving line. In the shadows of the trees and river cane thicket, Mattie Mae Blair was still the most beautiful woman he had ever seen.

"It's not bad," he said quietly.

She did not answer. She ducked her face away from him.

"I mean it," Vinnie said urgently. "When I first saw it, I thought it was, but close up, it's not, not at all."

"Don't say that, Vinnie," she whimpered. "I know how bad it is. I see it every day."

"Look at me," he said in a begging voice.

"No."

"Please."

"I can't."

"Yes, you can. Look at me."

She turned back to him. The thin, curving line was only a scratch.

"God, you're—beautiful," he whispered.

"Don't, Vinnie—"

"No, it's true. You are. There's nothing there. It's barely visible. I'm not lying. You're seeing things."

Mattie Mae touched her face with her fingers. She could feel the ridge of healed flesh.

"It's there, Vinnie."

"You remember what you told me once," he said. "You told me we were friends. You said we always would be."

"That was a long time ago, Vinnie."

192

"I thought it was a promise."

"It was. Then."

"You break promises?"

"Vinnie, look at me," she said bitterly. "You don't want me." She pushed her hair back, framing her face. Tears bubbled in her eyes. "Do you know how this happened? Do you know who did this?"

"No," Vinnie answered.

"He did it," Mattie Mae cried. "My lover, Vinnie. My New Orleans lover. I told him about you, Vinnie. I told him you were the only man who'd ever been decent to me and he went crazy, Vinnie. He always had a temper. I knew that, but I never thought he'd hurt me. But he did. And then he left, Vinnie. He left. He went back to Europe." She inhaled suddenly, swallowing a sob. She shouted, "You don't want me, Vinnie."

Vinnie leaned to her. He reached to touch her face, to touch the scar. A drop of water from Asa's Spring ran from his finger to her mouth. "Yes, I do," he said. "I do."

"Don't you see me, Vinnie? Don't you see how I look?"

"I see a small scar, that's all," he said.

"My God," she cried, "it's like somebody hit me with a saw. The plastic surgeons can't fix it, Vinnie. They've tried, but it still shows, and none of them know why. My mama calls it the Mark of Shame for all the wrong things I've done. She's right, Vinnie. It'll always be there."

He touched the scar again. "Funny, I don't see that at all. Maybe it just needed to be touched by somebody who wants you for all the good reasons." He leaned to her and put his lips on the scar and kissed it gently. "Now, it's gone," he said. "Look in the water. You'll see."

Mattie Mae turned to the water mirror and stared in wonder. A soft moan rose from her throat. She said, "Vinnie . . ."

The very righteous of Cuttercane—especially the women of the very righteous—had always believed Mattie Mae Blair had a ticket to hell due to her shameful behavior. The very non-righteous had believed she was a celebrity. The middle-roaders thought the squabble between the righteous and the non-righteous was more interesting than the fact that Mattie Mae had once taken off her clothes in the company of men.

When Mattie Mae and Vinnie were married in a private ceremony beneath the trees at Asa's Spring, the very righteous and the very non-righteous and the middle-roaders murmured among themselves that Vinnie was a forgiving man, or he was blind. Mattie Mae's face was still marked by a disfiguring cut that curled across her temple and cheek and chin, and only a thick coating of makeup made her presentable.

"Funny about that boy," the people said. "He swears he can't see a thing wrong with her face."

"He must of ducked his head in Asa's Spring."

"Either that or he's got the damnedest case of astigmatism on record. Wonder how he stands to look at her when they in bed?"

"He cuts off the light and just goes by feel, I'd said, and if that's the way he does it, he's got him the finest woman on Earth."

"She's something and that's a fact."

"I remember when she was fat as a sow hog. Remember her tagging along after her daddy, old Tanner Blair, before he up and run off?"

"Tanner was sorry as they come as a daddy, no doubt about it."

"Reckon it's true about her coming out of Asa's Spring with the body she's got now?"

"Lord, no. If that was it, every woman this side of the Mississippi would be down there."

"Yeah, but there's all them old stories about that place. If I thought they was true, I'd take my woman down there and throw her in. She don't have to look like Mattie Mae, but I wouldn't mind if she come out with some improvement."

"She did that, she might run off to one of them naked-girl clubs down in Atlanta."

"Could be. Maybe it's best just to leave things alone. They's not but one Mattie Mae Blair."

"That's the truth."

"Anyhow, I guess it just proves what my mama used to say."

"What's that?"

"It's not how you look that makes a difference; it's how people see you."